Three and One Make Five

by the same author

UNSEEMLY END
JUST DESERTS
MURDER BEGETS MURDER
TROUBLED DEATHS
DEADLY PETARD

RODERIC JEFFRIES

Three and One Make Five

An Inspector Alvarez novel

St. Martin's Press
New York

THREE AND ONE MAKE FIVE. Copyright © 1984 by Roderic Jeffries. All rights reserved. Printed in the United States of America. No part of this book may be used or reproduced in any manner whatsoever without written permission except in the case of brief quotations embodied in critical articles or reviews. For information, address St. Martin's Press, 175 Fifth Avenue, New York, N.Y. 10010.

Library of Congress Cataloging in Publication Data

Ashford, Jeffrey, 1926-
   Three and one make five.

   I. Title.
PR6060.E43T5   1984   823'.914   84-13249
ISBN 0-312-80240-4

First published in Great Britain by William Collins Sons & Co. Ltd.

First U.S. Edition

10 9 8 7 6 5 4 3 2 1

CHAPTER 1

Alvarez looked in the mirror and knew fresh sadness as he checked that his black tie was neat. Then he left the bedroom and went downstairs. Dolores, as crisply smart as ever, her strikingly handsome face expressing a sadness as great as his, came out of the kitchen. Few Mallorquins had heard of Donne but, being islanders of peasant stock, they knew the meaning of his words, 'Any man's death diminishes me . . .'

'Are you off now?' she asked.

He nodded.

'Poor, poor María,' she murmured.

Yet, he thought, it was only two days ago since María and Pedro had been one of the happiest couples on the island. His mind slipped back to January and the night of Revetla de San Sebastià when almost every street in the village built a bonfire on which was set a foguera. Pedro's tableau had won third prize: all who saw it—with the exception of the judges—had been agreed that it should have won first prize. A couple, in traditional costume, were dancing: as was only right and proper, there was a decorous distance between them. But the man's expression was so lecherous that no one could mistake his intentions. Old Grandma Villanova, 91 years old, toothless and refusing to wear her false teeth, had cackled with laughter and said that Pedro was a lad and a half and María's stomach would very soon start to swell again . . .

He left. The house was set directly on the pavement and he crossed to his battered Seat 600, sat behind the wheel, and turned the key. Amazingly, the engine fired first time although for weeks it had been reluctant to start at all. The perversity of life, he thought bitterly: when he would have welcomed delay . . .

He drove to 15, Calle General Riera, Pedro and María's home. The men were in the first room: they stood and were restless to the point of constantly moving about, yet they seldom spoke to each other and then only briefly. Ramón, Pedro's younger brother, eyes red, came forward and he and Alvarez embraced. Then Ramón led him into the second room where the women were all sitting on chairs set around the walls: the shutters were closed and the women's faces were indistinct, but the constant quiet sobbing testified to their misery.

He went to where María sat and bent down and kissed her tear-damped cheek. She gripped his arms. Was she remembering that night of Revetla de San Sebastià when Pedro had laughed so much he'd begun to choke? The crack of the bangers as the kids let them off without thought to safety, the cheers as the bonfire was lit, the way the man had twisted towards his partner as the flames reached round him, and the shrill cry of Old Grandmother Villanova, who'd been drinking brandy with reckless enjoyment, that, typical male, he was determined to have his fun whatever happened . . .

María released him. Ramón touched his arm and he followed, up the stairs and into the first bedroom.

Pedro lay on the bed, an immaculately ironed sheet drawn up to his chest. Four candles burned by the bed, two on either side: María had lit one and each of his three children had lit one. At his feet was a single wreath. On the chest-of-drawers, on a black linen cloth, were a dozen framed photographs, all of Pedro with the exception of one, the largest, which was of him and María on their wedding-day. On the ground at the foot of the bed were a set of chisels and two saws, marking his trade in life.

Alvarez crossed himself, then closed his eyes. But in his mind he continued to see the long, narrow face, touched with sly humour even in death, and he wondered. Was there a final mystery? Or, despite all the teachings of the church, had Pedro merely ceased to be? He opened his eyes, looked for the last time at Pedro, then left, followed by Ramón. He passed through the room of women to the room of men, where he leaned against one of the walls.

Plans for a new HQ building for the guardia civil in Llueso had, it was said by some, already been approved and the site had been bought: the new HQ was to be spacious, air-conditioned, and centrally heated. There were to be attached, luxurious quarters for married men. One or two of the optimists even went on to claim that completion date was set for only a year ahead. Others, however, more experienced in the workings of Spanish bureaucracy, doubted even an intention to consider the possibility of studying the problem of the working and living conditions of the members of the guardia civil: such pessimists accepted the certainty that they would continue for the foreseeable future to work in conditions of such overcrowding that quite often a man found himself writing out someone else's report.

Much to everyone's annoyance, an annoyance exacerbated by the fact that, being a civil servant he shouldn't have been in the post anyway, Alvarez had a room to himself on the first floor. Still, as he always claimed, in his very demanding job a man needed privacy if he were to work efficiently and effectively.

He leaned over and pulled open the bottom right-hand drawer of the desk to bring out a bottle and a glass. The phone rang. He ignored it and poured himself out a very large brandy. The ringing ceased. He settled back in his chair and drank and wondered why one man was taken and another was left. He'd known Pedro for twenty-five years: he'd been to the wedding and to each of the three christenings: he was godfather to little María . . .

The phone rang again. He stared at it with dislike, but eventually reached out and lifted the receiver.

'Is that Inspector Alvarez?'

Only one woman spoke as if her mouth were full of unripe plums, Superior Chief Salas's secretary. 'Yes, señorita.'

'There has been a fatal car crash on the road to the south of the monastery of San Miguel. Only the one car was involved and it seems probable that the driver, an Englishman, was under the influence of alcohol.' She sniffed loudly. 'The facts appear to be straightforward, but the woman with whom he was living'—she sniffed even more loudly—'has raised certain queries. She states that an hour before the crash he was perfectly sober and although there was a broken bottle of whisky in the car, there was no bottle in it when he left home and in any case he had not been drinking whisky for many years. You are to check to see whether there's cause for a full investigation.'

'The monastery at San Miguel, señorita, is not within my department.'

'Superior Chief Salas said he imagined you would raise that point. However, in view of the fact that you have had considerable experience in dealing with matters involving foreigners, he is directing you to investigate the case even though it lies in another department.'

'Señorita, I would be most grateful if someone else could deal with it. A very great friend of mine has just died . . .'

She said she was very sorry to hear that and then added, with all the moral certainty of someone who was not being called upon to show such fortitude, that there were times when duty had to come before sentiment.

CHAPTER 2

The monastery of San Miguel lay in the mountain range of the Sierra de Puig de Mas, to the north of the central plain, and it was built on a crest, as near to heaven as the builders could ever have reasonably hoped to get in their mortal state — the crests of higher mountains nearby had all proved to be too jagged and precipitous. The surrounding valleys were boulder-strewn and inhospitable and even the pine trees did not grow freely. Those few tourists who forsook the overcrowded beaches and drove here saw a land so different from the one they had left that they were bewildered and, quite often, uneasy, feeling as if their world of mindless play had somehow come under threat.

A road wound round the north side of the mountain and skirted the Garganta Verde. It had a spectacular setting. The gorge was so deep that only at noon in the height of the summer did sunshine ever reach its floor, and its sides were frequently almost sheer: over the centuries, rain had striated the rock face and now it looked as if some forgotten race of giants had drilled it for a reason it had become impossible to imagine. A few pine trees, roots somehow drawing sustenance from the rock, clung to the sides and there were infrequent clumps of weed grasses, dried brown and brittle by the heat. On the floor of the gorge there was a jumble of gnarled trees, bushes, and weeds, a sharp contrast to the poverty of the walls. Above both, riding the thermals, one could often see a black vulture, as graceful in flight as it was clumsy on the ground.

Like so many roads away from the centre of tourism, the edges of the one which skirted the gorge were not protected by stone copings or armco barrier and any misjudgement could have fatal consequences. They had been fatal for the driver of the Renault 18 which now lay, its roof crumpled down on to the seats, its wheels pointing skywards, half-way down the south side of the gorge, at rest on a wide ledge of rock.

Alvarez walked past the parked patrol car of the traffic police and went almost up to the edge of the road and looked down. Immediately, he experienced the stomach-churning terror of altophobia.

'That's the second one this year,' said the uniform policeman. 'Sometimes you wonder if they've ever driven before. Back in March three Germans in a Citroën went over the edge half a kilometre along and when they ended up you couldn't tell what had been car and what had been human.'

Alvarez felt as if he were being pulled gently but inexorably into the void by some unseen power and it needed all his will-power to break the spell and move backwards.

'You look like you don't go for heights,' said the policeman, a shade superciliously.

'Never did,' muttered Alvarez.

'They don't do anything to me. I reckon it's all in the mind.'

'So my mind prefers firm ground.'

They were standing in full sunshine and Alvarez was beginning to sweat from the heat. He moved a couple of metres to his right, into the shade of an evergreen oak. 'Is it certain Clarke was on his own?'

'Must have been. If there'd been anyone in the car with him, they'd not have got out, that's for sure.'

'Have you turned up anyone who saw or heard the accident?'

'It's not the centre of Palma here, you know.'

Alvarez looked down the road to the point where, fifty

metres on, it rounded a spur of rock. There would always be a certain amount of traffic, but it would never be great and a long time could pass between vehicles. 'How far away's the nearest house?'

'A couple of kilometres back, so they won't be of any help . . . Look, what's got you so concerned?'

'He was living with a woman and she swears he can't have been tight and that there wasn't a bottle of whisky in the car an hour earlier when he left home. On top of that, he didn't like whisky.'

'If he wasn't tight, why'd he leave the braking for so long?'

Alvarez looked up the road towards a right-hand turn two hundred metres away. The black rubber lines, marking panic braking, only started twenty metres from the edge of the road. They suggested that the driver had come round the corner fast and the car had gathered speed on the downhill run: then, too late, he'd realized he'd built up too much speed for the next corner and he'd braked, so fiercely that the car had gone into a dry skid which had taken it over the edge. What but alcohol would so fatally impair a driver's reactions on a road which was so obviously potentially dangerous?

'I searched the car,' said the policeman, 'and whatever his woman says there's a smashed bottle of whisky in it, all mixed up with a one-franc piece. If you don't believe me, go down and look for yourself.' He noted the expression on Alvarez's face and added jeeringly: 'I'll hold your hand on the way down.'

Thirty years before, the bay hadn't officially had a name although the locals had always referred to it as Bahia Mocamba. Low hills surrounded and led down to it, leaving between them a funnel of ever-widening flat, rocky soil. Only one dirt-track had passed through the land and this had not been used very much: the farmers and their families had been known as dour and inhospitable—in fact, they had merely been sturdily independent. Then the valley and its sandy beach had been 'discovered' by developers and the dirt-track became a wide metalled road which carried earth movers, bulldozers, cranes, and concrete mixers. Electricity advanced over the hills, to be followed immediately by the telephone. Fields vanished under concrete and the shoreline rose into eight- and ten-storey blocks of flats and hotels. At night, coloured lights advertised discothèques and, after the precipitate arrival of the permissive age, topless bars. Many men became rich. But the bee eaters no longer arrived in May to fill the air with their whistling calls and flashes of brilliant colours.

Clarke's house was in an up-market urbanización which was spread out over the lower slopes of one of the hills to the north of the valley. The garage and parking area in front were at a lower level than the house and to reach the front door one had to climb several stone steps. These caused Alvarez to breathe far too heavily and they reminded him just how out of condition he was.

He rang the front doorbell. A heavily built, middle-aged woman, wearing an apron over a patterned cotton frock, hair swept tightly back into a bun, opened the door and said in Mallorquin: 'What d'you want?'

'I'd like a word with Señorita Newcombe. Cuerpo General de Policia.'

'You know about the señor?'

He nodded.

'Then don't you understand she's not in a state to see anyone? She had to identify the body. It's been terrible for her.'

'Of course it has,' he answered, with obvious sympathy.

'Then come back another time.'

'I'm sorry, but I must speak to her now. I'll be as brief as it's possible.'

'She's already said all she's got to say.'

'Señora, I have to hear her story from herself.'

She studied him, her chunky face expressing uncertainty and then she pulled the door fully open. 'I suppose you'd best come in. But señor . . . be kind.'

She led him across a square hall and into a large sitting-room. After she'd left, he crossed to the French windows and stepped out on to the patio, which was shaped in a semi-circle and ringed with attractive wrought-iron railings. Being well up on the side of the hill, the view was magnificent, stretching across the town to the bay, with its enclosing hills, and the open sea beyond. But the drop immediately beyond the patio was sheer and this gave the effect of being suspended in mid-air so that he was immediately affected by vertigo. He hurriedly returned inside, cursing his weakness.

Calmer, he examined the sitting-room more closely than before. The furniture was Spanish and of good quality: the two large carpets looked, to his untutored eyes, to be Persian: four paintings hung on the walls and he tentatively identified one of them as being by a Mallorquin artist whose work was now commanding very high prices: to the right of the open fireplace was a stacked music centre, to the left, on a double table, a large colour TV and a video: beyond the music centre was a long bookcase, four shelves high, filled with books. Plenty of money, he thought.

He briefly heard footsteps, staccato on the tiled hall floor, and then Tracey Newcombe entered. In many ways he was an old-fashioned prude and so he believed that while it was natural for men to sow their wild oats ladies, to remain ladies, must sow nothing but decorum. Because Tracey had been living with Clarke, he had automatically thought of her as a whore. Now, face to face, he was astonished to discover that his assumption had been totally wrong.

She was tall and wore a printed cotton shirt and jeans that admitted to, but did not underline, a graceful figure. She had light, curly red hair, cut short and sufficiently unruly that however much she brushed it she still looked as if she'd just stepped in from a windswept moor. Her eyes were cornflower blue and set wide apart, at times giving her a slightly quizzical expression: her nose almost turned up at the tip: her mouth was made for laughing: her chin was both round and square, even if that was impossible. Her face could never be truly described as beautiful, yet it would be remembered long after the memory of a truly beautiful face was gone.

He said in English: 'I am very sorry, señorita, to have to trouble you at such a sad time.'

She nodded, crossed to the fireplace and stood in front of this, her hands clasped.

'Are you able to answer a few questions?'

'I suppose so,' she answered dully, her voice holding an accent which he could not place.

'Why not sit down?'

She unlocked her hands and went over to one of the armchairs. 'What is it you want to know?'

'What exactly happened yesterday morning and why you believe it was not just a most unfortunate accident?'

She was silent for so long that he was about to prompt her when she suddenly said: 'We were driving to Palma in the afternoon. Roger was going to see the dentist. After that we were having a picnic supper on Puig Craix. I was making the ham sandwiches when the policeman came here and told me what had happened. I remember, when the doorbell rang I was just telling myself everything would be all right in the end . . .' She stopped.

'Was something wrong, señorita?'

She ignored the question. 'Roger didn't really like picnics. He said one always got so sticky. That always made me laugh. I mean, half the fun of picnics is getting

sticky . . . But I said we had to have one. You see, I was hoping . . . Christ, I need a drink!' She stood, gestured with her hands, crossed to a mobile cocktail cabinet in the far corner of the room. She opened up the top flaps and this action, through counterweights, brought up a shelf on which were several bottles and half a dozen glasses.
'Would you like something?'
'A coñac would be very pleasant.'
She poured out two brandies. 'Do you like soda and ice?'
'Just ice, thank you.'
She added soda to one glass. 'I'll go through to the kitchen and get some ice.' She left.

Silently, he cursed the world which brought bitter sorrow to so many. Priests often said that sorrow ennobled the soul, but he had never believed this was anything other than an attempt to explain away something that was all too clearly unmerciful.

She returned with an insulated ice bucket. Using tongs, she dropped three ice cubes into one glass and then came over to hand the drink to him. When she'd added ice to the second glass, she returned to the armchair. 'My dad won't have alcohol in the house. When my sister and me had drinks out, we had to suck peppermints before we returned back home. Mum always knew why we'd been eating peppermints, but Dad never seemed to guess. Or maybe he took care not to. He was always strict, but he was human.'

'Which part of Britain do you live in, señorita?'

'New Zealand. South Island. Out in the foothills of the McKerrows, the most beautiful country in the world. When I remember it, there's a lump in my throat the size of a house and I wonder just what in the hell I'm doing here . . . I needed to go for a picnic on Puig Craix because it's like Barrats Hill, on Dad's place: on its own and kind of sugar loaf. When I was a kid I used to climb to the top and think myself queen of the world and when anything really serious went wrong I went up there and petitioned for it to be put right. Not that I can remember who I was petitioning. Maybe it was my fairy godmother.' There was a brief, forlorn smile that flickered and then was gone. 'God, that's a whole lifetime ago!

'I'd never told Roger about Barrats Hill because that was a personal secret, but I'm sure he understood there was some special reason for driving to Puig Craix and it wasn't just to have a picnic. That's why he agreed to go when he'd so much rather have eaten here or gone to a restaurant . . . The ham sandwiches I was making are in the fridge now. After the policeman had gone, I wrapped them up in film because I just couldn't believe him and I was so sure Roger would be back and we'd be off . . .' She stared into space for several seconds, then drank.

'Señorita, it cannot seem to you now that time will heal the wounds, but it will. I promise you that.'

She said angrily: 'How in the hell can you know what time will do?'

'Many years ago, my fiancée was killed by a car,' he said quietly. 'Her wedding-dress had been made and although I never saw it I know it would have made her the most beautiful woman in the world . . . In time, my memories of her became precious, not open knives. Last night, Pedro, a very great friend of mine, died. Now, my memories of him are open knives, but gradually they also will become precious.'

Tears welled out of her eyes and down her cheeks. 'God, I wish . . . .' Her tone became almost fierce. 'We both need Barrats Hill.'

'Señorita?'

'Will you drive us to Puig Craix?'

He hesitated, but only for a second. If he could help ease a little of her sorrow, perhaps she could help ease a little of his. 'Of course,' he said.

★

The hill rose out of the island's central plain with all the suddenness and symmetry of a child's drawing. Pine trees grew up its sides for two-thirds of its height, then the rock became bare except for the occasional clump of weed grass or cistus bush. For two hundred years there had been a hermitage on the crown, but in the twentieth century few men felt the call and the last resident had died nineteen years before. There was only a mule track leading up to the hermitage and largely because of this — to convert the buildings into a tourist restaurant would, in the absence of a road, be ridiculous — the buildings had been left to decay.

They reached the summit and sat just outside the shadows of a square building whose roof had fallen in. For a while neither spoke, Tracey because her thoughts were obviously far away, Alvarez because he was so short of breath, his heart was thumping, and his legs were shaking from exhaustion; if the climb had been only fifty metres longer, he felt certain he would have collapsed.

Tracey, who now lay on her stomach, her head resting on her crossed arms, broke the silence. 'I left home because I couldn't stand things any longer. Life had to be something more than doing the same thing day after day. Mary, my sister, never ever felt like that. She's always hated change. She's married to a bloke she's known since she was a kid and if she was given one wish it would be for things to go on just as they are. Sometimes, like now, I wish to God I could have been like her. But what should life be? Should it be just living and not being hurt too often, or the excitement of exploring but being hurt over and over again?'

'I don't know, señorita.'

'For Pete's sake, I'm Tracey.' She turned her head round until she could look at him. 'And now you're going to tell me your name?'

'Enrique.'

Enrique — is that Henry? I've always like Henry: it's the name of kings — but you're much too nice to be a king. You're one of the kindest men I've ever met.'

In his embarrassment, he smiled briefly.

'You must do that more often: it makes you stop looking sad and as if you've learned that nothing's real, it's all an illusion . . . I'm talking absolute nonsense and d'you know why? It's because we're on Barrats Hill and everything that's said is secret so I can be as nonsensical as I want. You do know it's all secret here, don't you, Enrique?'

'Yes.'

'That's why I'm going to tell you . . .'

'Tell me what?'

Her momentary vivaciousness was gone and her voice became once more sad. 'Something I don't want to confess even to myself . . . Things were often difficult between me and Roger. We kept having rows. They started quite a time back, when he went to Liechtenstein and wouldn't take me. I accused him of going after another woman . . . When he came back he'd brought me such a lovely present I said it was conscience money . . . Then things kind of came all right again. But we still had rows. He was undemonstrative and only a fortnight ago I shouted at him that love had to be a two-way operation. I don't think he understood what I was really trying to say . . . I remembered home and all of a sudden I wanted to be back where nothing changes and tomorrow's going to be the same as today. To tell the truth, I'd decided to leave him if our picnic here didn't really change things . . . And then yesterday morning . . . It's made me feel . . .' She stopped.

'As if you were somehow to blame?'

'Perhaps he didn't have any doubts and wasn't fed up with me, but knew I was feeling like I was and that upset him so much that he did go and drink too much. And because he'd drunk so much, he crashed . . . . So if I hadn't almost decided to leave him, maybe it wouldn't have happened.'

'After any tragedy it's always possible to look back and say perhaps this and perhaps that and to work out how the tragedy could have been avoided. But if at the time you were doing what you thought was right and weren't trying to hurt someone, then in truth it couldn't have been avoided.'

'I didn't want to hurt him: I was trying all I could not to. I thought maybe leaving him would make it easier for both of us . . .'

'Then you're not in any way to blame for his death, Tracey.'

She shifted her head on to her left arm, stretched out with her right and briefly touched his forearm in a gesture of gratitude.

CHAPTER 3

Alvarez reached his office at five past nine and the telephone rang before he had had time to sit and recover his breath from the walk up the stairs.

'Alvarez,' said Superior Chief Salas, in his typically abrupt manner, 'I have been waiting for your report.'

'Which report, señor?'

'Good God, man, are you still asleep? On the car crash near the monastery of San Miguel, of course.'

'Well, as a matter of fact . . . I haven't yet been able to investigate the matter.'

'What the devil do you mean?'

'When I saw Señorita Newcombe I decided she was much too distressed to be questioned.'

'And since when have you been qualified, or required, to determine a witness's state of mind?'

'It was just that knowing there was no very great urgency in the matter . . .'

'No very great urgency? Will you never learn that there's a very great urgency in every case until it's solved?'

'What I was trying to say . . .'

'But not succeeding. You're to return and question the woman this morning and kindly remember you are not being called upon to pass any judgement whatsoever on her mental state. Is that quite clear?'

'Quite clear, señor. As a matter of fact, I did tell her . . .'

Salas cut the connection.

Alvarez sighed as he replaced the receiver. People from Madrid seemed always to believe that each minute of every day had to be turned inside out instead of being left to mature with dignity.

He looked at his watch. He'd arranged to meet Tracey again this morning — as he would have told Salas had he been allowed to — but there was no point in leaving for another three-quarters of an hour. And three-quarters of an hour was too short a time to start any other work. He relaxed. He closed his eyes the better to do so.

The front door of Ca'n Renaldo was opened by Tracey. 'Come on in, Enrique,' she said, as she held the door fully open. 'Let's have some coffee — come on into the kitchen and talk while I fix up the machine. Matilde doesn't come in on a Wednesday, so I'm on my own.'

He followed her into the tiled, elaborately equipped kitchen. She crossed to the gas stove and picked up a saucepan which she half filled at the sink. 'The water's supposed to be perfectly drinkable, but Dad always told us that if you boil all water and milk and throw away all liquor, you'll live to be a hundred. I don't want to be a hundred, so I just boil water.'

'Didn't you say your father is a farmer?'

'Sheep. Thousands of the stupid animals. Dad's a first-class sheepman,' she said proudly. 'Gets top prices for his fleeces and lambs.' She put the saucepan on the stove and lit the gas. 'But if only just once he'd become curious about the world beyond the farm . . . Am I sounding like a prize bitch?'

He was startled and showed this.

'Well, he's the most wonderful father yet all I seem to be able to do is criticize him. He didn't like me leaving home, but when Mum said it would do me good to get rid of the flicks in my feet, he stopped arguing and gave me the money to travel. I suppose my real trouble now is, he's been so kind he makes me feel a bit ashamed of myself . . . Tell me something. Why the hell is it that normally I keep my problems to myself, yet ever since I met you yesterday I've been going on and on as if you were an agony aunt?'

'An agony aunt?'

'One of those women in a magazine one writes to with all the questions one's too ashamed to ask one's parents . . . And before you came here this morning I was full of good resolutions about not bothering you any more and thanking you for everything you did for me yesterday.'

'You helped me every bit as much as I helped you.'

'The perfect mutual aid society! . . . I'll confess something. Until now, I've always thought the people on this island hated us foreigners.'

'You needed help.'

'Are you saying that if I hadn't, then you would have disliked me as a matter of principle?'

'You have to understand, Tracey. We're a very small island and always used to lead our own lives, poor as we were. Then the foreigners came, first in their hundreds, then their thousands, then their hundreds of thousands. Everything became changed. And because we suddenly were better off and had more, we learned to want still more: the young grew up to despise their parents for being illiterate, to drive cars instead of riding bicycles, to walk in the streets with their arms about their girls when in the past not even married couples would have behaved so badly.'

'Progress!'

The coffee was made and she filled two cups. As she put these on a tray and then picked out of a cupboard a silver sugar bowl, she said: 'Earlier on, I suddenly realized the strange fact that I won't be living here much longer. That got me to wondering who'll be using the kitchen? I hope she's happier than I've ended up being.'

'You don't imagine Señor Clarke will have left the house to you?'

'Not a chance and if there were I'd refuse it. No, he'll probably have left it to his wife.'

'He's married?'

'His wife lives back in England . . . You look shocked? I suppose this is the kind of change you so hate. And they're even bringing in divorce in Spain, aren't they? But Roger and Helen never could get on, so wasn't it better for them to part than live together and fight all the time?'

'I only know that when people can't get divorced, they usually learn to accept each other.'

'And be miserable.'

'Do we have a right to expect life to be happy? . . . Did you know he was married?'

'When I first met him, no. But when it became a question of moving in here with him, he told me. He was very straight like that. A lot of men would have kept their mouths tight shut.' She picked up the tray. 'Last night, I dreamt Roger and I were out in his boat and he told me we mustn't ever fight again. When I woke up I reached across the bed to touch him and promise I'd try not to be bitchy again and . . . and only when my hand met nothing did I remember.' She shivered. 'Am I going to dream like that a lot?'

'I expect so.'

'Did your dreams frighten you?'

'They made me very sad.' After Juana-María had died, he had often had dreams from which he had awoken with tears. He hoped her dreams were not so cruel.

She led the way through to the sitting-room. 'Shall we go out on to the patio?' She noticed his hesitation. 'Don't you like it in the sun?'

'It's not that,' he confessed. 'I'm one of those idiots who's scared of heights and out there I feel as if I'm on the edge of a precipice.'

'Then we stay in here.' She put the tray down on an occasional table. 'I'd never have suggested going to Puig Craix yesterday if you'd told me that . . . But it didn't seem to upset you?'

'The climb left me so exhausted I didn't have enough energy to be frightened.'

She smiled at him.

Ten minutes later, he said: 'I am sorry, Tracey, but I must ask you some questions.'

'Yes, I know.' Her expression tightened. 'All right, let's get it over and done with.'

'Do you know where the señor was driving to the day before yesterday? The road he was on when he crashed doesn't lead anywhere but the north coast and it would have taken him another three-quarters of an hour to get over the mountains and just as long to get back, yet he had a dentist's appointment in the afternoon.'

'I've no idea what he was doing there.'

'Does he have friends in Sa Calobra, or perhaps round the coast to the west?'

'He's never talked of anyone and certainly we've never gone anywhere in that direction. As a matter of fact, Roger didn't have many friends. He was a bit of a loner, really.'

'So you can't suggest why he was on that road?'

'Not unless the reason had something to do with the phone call.'

'What call was that?'

'I can't tell you except the phone rang and he answered it and when the call was over and I asked him who it had been, he shouted at me to mind my own business and stop prying into his life . . .' Her expression became strained. 'I've got quite a temper and that made me see red and . . . Well, we had a right old row.'

'Didn't he give any sort of a hint as to who the caller had been?'

'None at all.'

'What kind of a mood was he in before the call?'

'Very pleasant. We both were because, I suppose, we'd reached the point where we were consciously doing all we could to avoid any more trouble.'

'Then it was the telephone call which upset him?'

'It must have been.'

'Might it have upset him so much that he started drinking, without you realizing it?'

'I . . . I suppose that's possible. I mean, after the row we kept at arm's length until he left. But the drink's either in the cocktail cabinet, over there, or down in the cellar and I don't think he went near either. And after he'd gone, there wasn't a dirty glass anywhere around.'

'What exactly happened when he left?'

'By then I'd calmed down a bit and was telling myself I'd been a right royal bitch and was I deliberately twisting everything he said or did in order to find the justification for leaving him . . . I started feeling guilty, so when he went out of the house I followed. He backed the car out of the garage and I made him stop. I told him I was sorry, but he started shouting at me again, telling me I was always prying into his life . . . That made me forget all my good resolutions and I started shouting back . . . It's all so bloody sordid. Can't we forget it?'

'There's only a very little more I have to know. You told the police there wasn't a bottle of whisky in the car—how certain are you? Couldn't there have been a bottle in the boot or under one of the front seats?'

'I suppose there could have been—but why would anyone keep a bottle in the boot? What I meant was, when he drove away there wasn't a bottle on any of the seats. But don't you understand, he never drank whisky so he couldn't have drunk from the bottle the police said was found in the car.'

'Are you sure he didn't like it?'

'Of course I am. Damnit, I lived with him long enough to know what he did and didn't drink. He told me once, he used to drink it some years ago, but then he really caned himself on it once and after that he went right off it . . .' She stopped, gazed through one of the windows.

Alvarez rubbed his thickset chin. 'As far as you know, was there anyone who disliked him very much? Or was there anyone of whom he was afraid?'

'Why should he have been scared of anyone?'

'Don't you understand that if the crash wasn't an accident, which is what your evidence is really saying, then someone must have killed him deliberately.'

'My God! . . . I just never thought of it like that . . .'

He had obviously questioned her long enough and to continue might be to upset her too much. He stood. 'You have been very patient in answering all my questions which must have hurt so much. Thank you very much.'

'You're not going?' She began to fidget with the beading of the armchair. 'I . . . I was hoping you'd stay for lunch. I went out earlier to the butcher and bought two steaks which he promised would be really nice. I love steak. I was in Australia for several months and the steaks there . . . Oh hell, what's it matter what the steaks in Australia were like? Enrique, please stay. I thought last night would never end and until you came this morning it

was like living a nightmare. Don't leave me yet.'
He sat down.

Alvarez rang Palma in the morning and he listened with a sinking feeling to the plum-voiced secretary as she told him that Superior Chief Salas was in his office and would speak to him.

'What the devil's been happening? I expected to hear from you by lunch-time yesterday at the very latest.'

'Señor, Señorita Newcombe was still in a very distressed state and it was some considerable time before I was able to question her.'

'Well?'

'Although he'd once liked it, Señor Clarke had not drunk whisky for several years. When he drove away from his house on the morning he died, there was no bottle of whisky visible in the car. The señorita had no idea where he was driving to or who he was going to see. I specifically asked her about friends in Sa Calobra, since the road past the monastery leads there . . .'

'I am fully aware of where the road goes.'

'On that morning, he'd been in a good humour until there was a phone call but after this, when she asked him who it had been from, he became very angry. There doesn't seem any doubt but that the phone call was responsible for his journey.

'I asked her if she knew of anyone who might have had a motive for murdering him. She said there was no one.'

'She must have an idea who the call was from?'

'Apparently not.'

'Are you saying, then, that it was a highly significant call but we're unlikely ever to learn what that particular significance was?'

'Yes, señor.'

There was a short silence. 'If it upset him so much, when he drove away from the house he was still in a mentally disturbed state. Remembering that he then probably drank heavily, it's not difficult to understand how the crash occurred.'

'Señor, he hadn't touched whisky for several years . . .'

'The point I'm trying to make—in the face of difficulties—is that when a man is mentally disturbed he often behaves in an irrational manner. Clarke had once drunk whisky, so in his disturbed state he suddenly decided to drink it again.'

'But where did the bottle in the car come from?'

'I presume you asked the señorita whether there was any whisky in the house?'

'Er . . . No, señor.'

'Regrettable, but not surprising . . . Clearly, the bottle could have come from the house. Equally clearly, he could have stopped on his journey and bought it.' Salas's voice sharpened. 'Did it by any lucky chance occur to you to find out what happens to the estate now?'

'The señorita doesn't know for certain, but she believes everything goes to the wife, even though she and the señor have been living apart.'

'Then if it proves to be true that the señorita has no financial interest in Clarke's death, the case depends on whether or not he was drunk at the time of the crash.'

'I . . . I suppose so.'

'You sound uncertain. Have I proceeded too quickly for you to follow?'

'No, señor. It's just that . . . Well, I do wonder if everything really is quite as straightforward as it seems? I think we could be missing something important.'

'A thought with which, no doubt, you've become over familiar,' said Salas before cutting the connection.

The results of the PM reached Alvarez on a Friday. The deceased had had a blood alcohol ratio of 0.2—in other words he had, in lay terms, been in a state of marked drunkenness.

CHAPTER 4

By the first of July, the day temperature had risen to the middle nineties and there had been no rain for nine weeks. Where there was irrigation the land remained green, elsewhere it had turned brown. On the beaches the holidaymakers sunbathed, frequently to excess so that they needed medical attention: doctors and chemists regarded the July sun in the light of a second patron saint. The harbour of Puerto Llueso was filled with boats, ranging from twelve-foot speedboats to seventy-foot schooners, almost all owned by foreigners whose constant topic of conversation was the subject of how hard up they were. The sea-front cafés charged twice as much as was reasonable and memento shops succeeded in selling their stocks to foreigners who had obviously left any sense of judgement or taste at home.

Alvarez awoke and stared up at the ceiling of his bedroom, patterned by the light striking up through closed shutters, and he idly wondered if it were five o'clock yet? If so, he really ought to start thinking about getting up. The thought depressed him.

Downstairs, the telephone rang. Most calls were for him, but occasionally there was a private one so he waited for someone else to answer. The ringing continued. Dolores, he decided, was beginning to take life far too easily.

He sighed, swivelled round, stood, then reached for his trousers and put them on. From below came the sound of a door being banged and the clack of high heels on tiles and then the ringing finally stopped. He sat down once more.

'Enrique, it's for you.'

Wearily he stood and reached for his shirt.

'Hurry it up.'

He left and went downstairs.

Dolores, who was standing near the phone, said: 'If you drank less coñac after lunch, you'd be able to move a bit faster.'

Women never understood the simple fact that a man's digestion, which was a delicate subject, was aided by a little brandy.

The caller was the duty guard at the post. 'There's a woman here, asking for you.'

'Who is she?'

'How should I know?'

'What's she want?'

The guard laughed salaciously.

'She must have said something?'

'All she's said is she wants a word with you. God knows why!'

'Is she young, middle-aged, old?'

'A foreigner, far too young for an old man like you.'

Alvarez replaced the receiver.

'Is anything wrong?' asked Dolores.

'Just someone turned up at the station who wants to see me.'

'Then you won't wait for coffee?'

He yawned. 'Its not an emergency.'

The reception area was immediately inside the main entrance of the guardia post and here a guard sat behind a desk and, when he could find no alternative, dealt with inquiries from the public.

Alvarez stepped from the sun-blasted street into the comparative gloom and initially he couldn't see clearly.

'Hullo, Enrique,' said a woman.

He finally recognized her and the moment he did so he wondered how on earth he could have failed to identify her from her voice alone.

Tracey was wearing a gaily embroidered blouse, green jeans, and rope-soled sandals. The lines of sorrow and worry had gone and now she looked young, vital, and laughingly eager to live twenty-four hours a day.

She chuckled. 'Is it such a terrible shock to find it's me?'

'Of course not,' he protested, conscious that the guard at the desk, unable to understand what they were saying, was watching them with an interest which was based on a totally false and cynical assumption.

'I couldn't think of any way of finding you without coming here. I hope it's all right?'

'Of course it is . . . Would you like a coffee?'

'I'd love one.'

'Then let's go to the square.'

They walked to the doorway. 'If anyone wants you,' said the guard in Spanish, 'I'll tell 'em you're engaged.'

Alvarez, about to step outside, checked himself. 'She's a witness.'

'Yeah. But a witness to what?'

Tracey was waiting in the middle of the road and the sun was raising highlights in her curly hair. 'I can't tell you how wonderful it is to see you again, Enrique!'

'It's good for me, too.'

'But why so serious about it?' She laughed again and as they started along the road she seemed to be skipping rather than walking. 'Did you expect to see me again?'

'Not really. I thought you would be back on Barrats Hill.'

She shook her head and the highlights in her hair danced. 'Not yet.' She touched his left arm lightly and for a second. 'Not yet.'

Had she not returned home because she wanted to see him again first: was that what she was really saying? . . . What bloody fool ideas could come to a man, he thought angrily. Yet nothing could alter the fact that she had gone to all the trouble of looking him up . . .

They reached the end of the road and entered the square, both the geographical and spiritual centre of the village. Here, on land which sloped so that part had had to be built up, was held the vegetable market on Sunday, the livestock market on Tuesday, and the fish market every day: here were held the fiesta dances: here the old men sat out and through rheumy eyes watched the world slide by: here, the foreign residents drank and exchanged malicious gossip, wounding criticism, and ridiculous rumours.

They climbed the stone steps up to the raised section, past flower-beds, and went over to a table set in the shadow of a plane tree. A waiter came across and she asked for coffee while he ordered coffee and a brandy.

As she looked around the square, with the eager interest of a tourist, he studied her and knew a sudden pain that anyone could be so young and alive. Then she turned back to look directly at him and he said hurriedly, to try and hide his thoughts: 'How have things been?'

'Not so bad . . . That's a lie. They became bloody difficult.' She opened her handbag and brought out a pack of cigarettes. 'The problems were too much and I've started smoking again. Just no will-power.' She offered the pack and he took a cigarette, then struck a match for both of them.

'The real trouble was,' she said, 'Roger's wife arrived. God knows how he ever came to marry her. Frightfully, frightfully refined in superior style—and no one beats the British at that.'

'Did she inherit the house?'

'She did. But apparently there's little beyond that so she's not rich, as she probably hoped. And being a malicious bitch, that makes me feel good . . . But enough of my miseries. What's been happening to you?'

'Nothing changes here.'

'You're lucky. I sometimes wonder who really leads the happier life, me or my sister? I think I'd go mad, stuck in the middle of thousands of sheep, yet then a wife wouldn't come along and at a moment's notice kick me out of the house I've lived in for eighteen months.'

'That hurt, didn't it?' he said with deep sympathy.

'Yes, it did, even though I knew it had to come. Maybe things had started to go sour between me and Roger, but we'd still had some wonderful times together and the house had been our home. I wish . . . When things go wrong, Enrique, I'm like a little girl and I start wishing they could all be changed and made right after all.'

'That's why you've still got Barrats Hill.'

'It's funny how well you understand me.' She saw his expression and smiled. 'And now I've embarrassed you, although I can't see why!'

The waiter returned and put two cups of coffee, a jug of milk, two packets of sugar, and a glass of brandy down on the table, together with the bill. As he left, a car on the north side of the square backfired and several pigeons lifted off the high roof of the church with clapping wings.

She spoke abruptly, almost belligerently. 'I've rented a flat down in the port.' She tore off the corner of one of the sugar packets.

'D'you mean in Puerto Llueso?'

'Everyone said how lovely it still was and when I was kicked out of Roger's house I drove over to see if that was true. There was a notice of a flat to let right on the front, so I took it. Maybe we can see something of each other?' She poured the sugar into her coffee.

At eleven years of age, Juan was precocious, but perhaps no more so than the average Mallorquin boy who was spoiled from birth. He studied Alvarez. 'Uncle, you're not talking as much as usual. D'you think you're dying?'

'That's quite enough of that,' said Dolores sharply.

'Is Uncle dying?' asked Isabel, Juan's younger sister, with considerable interest.

Jaime chuckled as he pushed the bottle of wine across the table to Alvarez. 'Here, finish this in one last booze before you peg out.'

'Will you please stop this nonsense,' snapped Dolores.

'But Uncle's been looking at nothing and he didn't have a second helping of arroz brut,' persisted Juan.

Dolores pursed her lips. It was quite true, Alvarez had not had a second helping of her delicious arroz brut. 'Are you not feeling well, Enrique?'

'Never felt better,' he replied, as heartily as possible. He picked up the bottle and refilled his tumbler.

'I bet I know the trouble,' said Jaime suddenly. 'It's a woman!'

Alvarez flushed.

'Don't be ridiculous,' said Dolores, her tone more questioning than admonitory.

'I tell you, when a bloke's off his grub he's either dying or starving.'

'That's quite enough of that, in front of the children,' she said, now angry.

Juan was puzzled. 'If you're starving, you must be dying.'

Jaime began to explain. 'There's two kinds of starving for a men and one of 'em's a sight more painful than the other . . .' He stopped abruptly when he saw Dolores's expression.

'Are we going to get anything more to eat?' asked Juan.

'Eating and drinking, that's all this family every thinks about,' she snapped.

'Would you rather I started thinking of something else?' Jaime asked, winking at Alvarez as he spoke.

Alvarez lay in bed and listened to the low, bee-like hum of traffic on the main road to the port. What had she said as they'd parted? 'You will come and see me in my little flat, won't you? Promise?'

Of course, she was lonely: lonely and still suffering from the shock of the death of Clarke. And like any other lonely person, she was eager to make contact with someone she knew, even if he were twice her age, in the hopes that her loneliness would thereby be eased . . .

A woman as vivacious as she would very soon make friends and therefore cease to be lonely. Then, surely, she'd not want to bother with someone who was at best no more than a very casual acquaintance . . .

Why had she come to Puerto Llueso instead of returning to New Zealand? Because she'd been told the bay was so lovely? It was, but so were many bays. And if it had been natural beauty for which she'd been searching, hadn't she called her own country the most beautiful in the world?

CHAPTER 5

Alvarez parked his car by the side of a palm and climbed out. Immediately to his left the sand—all imported by lorry because the original, very much smaller beach had been shingle—ran down to the water. A large number of people were sunbathing and many of the women, including some who should have been old enough to know better, were topless. He thought of Tracey topless and he hated the imagined men who goggled at her breasts.

He stared across the road at the buildings—some old, made from stone, and no more than two storeys high, some modern, made from concrete, and up to six stories high, and identified the one in which she had her flat. Someone, and it was almost certainly she, was sitting out on the small patio. He put his hand in his trouser pocket and jiggled the coins in it. At this time of the year the port was filled with money: foreign plated Mercedes, Porsches, Jaguars, BMWs, and Range Rovers, were almost as commonplace as Spanish plated Seats: in the harbour were boats, the upkeep alone of which would come to more than his annual salary: why should Tracey really want to have anything to do with him . . . ?

He crossed the road. The old fisherman's cottage had been divided in two and rickety wooden stairs led up. He climbed these, very conscious of the creaking of the treads which were so clearly heralding his arrival. His head rose above the level of the patio floor. Tracey sat in a canvas and wooden chair and she was wearing sunglasses which gave her face more than the usual dash of anonymity—and added a sharpnesss. She watched him appear, segment by segment, but said nothing until he reached the top step. 'What a surprise.' No one had ever sounded less surprised. 'You've finally remembered where I'm living and so, having nothing better to do, you're visiting.'

He was bewildered by her sarcastic coldness. 'You said to come and see you here . . .'

'There was no need to put yourself out like this.'

'I came because I wanted to see you.'

'So much that it's taken you four days to get here?'

'Well, I . . .'

'I'm sure you've been very busy. So don't think that just for my sake you ought to stay around for a bit.'

'Tracey, I . . .' He gesticulated with his hands.

'Yes?' she said, with the sweet reasonableness of someone who was about to deliver the coup de grâce.

'I don't understand.'

'English can be a difficult language, can't it?'

'But didn't you want me to come and see you?'

'Only if you wanted to come. And you can hardly claim that when it's taken you four days to arrive.'

'But I was nervous about coming.'

'Why?'

'I didn't know if you really wanted to see me again.'
'You can't be that thick.'
'It's the truth.'
'Why the hell d'you think I called at the guardia post?'
'I was hoping it meant . . . But then I remembered how old I am . . .'
'Christ, you're not Methuselah . . . Are you telling the truth? That you honest to God didn't know whether I really wanted to see you again just because you're a bit older than me?'
'Many years,' he murmured sadly.
'Enrique,' she said, and her voice had suddenly softened, 'you're one goddamn fool! D'you think I care how old you are? When I learned Roger was dead I started feeling I was to blame. Then the policeman asked me questions and it was all part of the day's work for him; he wasn't rude, or anything like that, but he didn't know how to be sympathetic. And as soon as he learned I wasn't Mrs Roger Clarke, he was wondering if I'd like a fresh bedmate. You were so different. You didn't give a damn who I was and you were so sympathetic it was like finding an old friend. And when I asked you to take me to Puig Craix you understood immediately and took me, never mind what else you had to do . . . Then, when the bitch of Roger's wife kicked me out of the house I felt all cold and lonely again and part of me was desperate for help. I could have flown back to NZ, but the family wasn't what I needed. I needed you. So I came here. I found this flat and afterwards drove up to the village to tell you about it so you could come here and make me feel warm and wanted again. I waited and waited, but you didn't come and the cold and the loneliness got worse and worse until I hated you because it seemed that all your help and sympathy hadn't really meant much after all . . . And now you tell me that the only reason you weren't down here immediately is because you thought I'd be worried

because you're a bit older than me! ... You need ... I'm damned if I know what you need!'
'I am certainly one goddamn fool.'
'You can say that again, in letters five feet high. And I'm one goddamn bitch and you can say that again, in letters ten feet high . . . Why didn't you belt me hard a moment ago when I was being so bitchy?' She paused, then said: 'Even the suggestion upsets you, doesn't it?'
He nodded. 'I don't like even joking about hitting a woman.'
'Of course you don't. Tell me, does one have to suffer a lot before one can be so emotionally kind and generous as you?'
He didn't try to answer.
'Come and sit down and stop looking as if you might decide to leave after all.' She pointed to a second patio chair. 'You'll have to learn to blame my red hair.'
'For what?' he asked as he sat.
'For my being such a bad-tempered bitch at times. Dad always said I came to the boil quicker'n anyone else he knows: although Mum told him he'd only got to look in a mirror to see someone as quick.' She spoke thoughtfully. 'Mum also said something else I often think about. Sharp people lead sharp lives. I've never decided whether she thinks that's a good thing, or not . . . Pour out some drinks. We're going to celebrate.'

It was dark. Before them stretched the bay, ringed by mountains which, traced out by moonlight, became possessed of a distant, insubstantial quality: on the water, the moonlight was a splintered shaft of gold. To their right, a woman with a small but true voice was singing softly to the accompaniment of a guitar. Some traffic passed along the road in front of them, but the noise failed to disturb the image of peace.
'Sometimes, like now,' she said, 'I feel it's time to die.'

'What?' he said, startled.

'Can anywhere, any time, be more wonderful than here, now? I'm floating in happiness . . . How could I be luckier than to die now, when everything's just perfect?'

He remembered Juana-María. Everything had been just perfect for her until the split second before her death, when the car had crashed into her and flung her against the wall. Yet whatever her death had been for her, for him it had been a tragedy that was dimmed by time, but never wholly expunged.

'What are you thinking, Enrique?'

'That things are never perfect for everyone. If you died right now, would your family consider your death was right?'

'I'm not worrying about them. Haven't you understood something about me yet? I'm a very selfish person.'

'Don't be ridiculous.'

'It's true . . . But just for once, I will consider someone else. You can die with me.'

'You are very generous.'

She chuckled.

'Tracey, I think I really ought to leave and return home.'

'You can't break up everything so early: stay in wonderland.'

'It isn't early and I have to work tomorrow.'

'How boring can life get? . . . Well, you're not going until you've promised me something. All right?'

'All right.'

'Before you've heard what it is you've got to promise? You could get yourself into terrible trouble like that . . . You're to promise you'll come and see me tomorrow.'

'You didn't have to make me promise to do that.'

'How do I know you won't start getting stupid thoughts again?'

'I probably shall.' He did not explain that his stupidity

would be taking a different form.
'Bring a costume so we can go swimming.'
'I'm not a good swimmer.'
'Well, I am. So you'd better prepare yourself to be ducked. I've decided something very important. You're too serious and you've got to learn to relax and stop worrying.'
'But if you start ducking me, surely I will worry even more?'
'Not the way I go about it.'
'I'm glad I finally plucked up the courage to come here, Tracey.'
'The man says he needed courage!'
'It is true: I did.'
'And I'm glad too, Enrique: very glad,' she said, with sudden seriousness. 'Every moment I'm with you, Roger moves further away.'
He stood. 'I will come as soon as I can tomorrow.'
'And I promise not to be bitchy again: at least, not nearly as bitchy as I've been this evening. Let's blame Roger's wife for that — so bloody puritanically superior . . . I wonder if Simon Allen's wife was like her and that's why Roger never saw them?'
'Who's she?'
'Simon was a friend of Roger's. The poor devil drowned off Playa Turra last night. I saw the news in the local rag this morning and recognized him by the photo . . . And now I've done the unforgivable and introduced the outside world which is so cruel and harsh. I'm a born escapist, Enrique. I want life to be all sun and no rain. So tomorrow we forget the outside world and live in our own inner one where everyone's always happy. Right?'

CHAPTER 6

Alvarez stepped out of his house into the harsh sunshine and crossed the pavement to his car. He unlocked the driving door and sat, but did not immediately start the engine. Last night, Tracey had said something to him to which, at the time, he had given no further thought: but this morning he'd woken up and remembered and begun to wonder. A man called Allen had drowned on Monday. On the face of things, nothing extraordinary in that. Tragically, holidaymakers swam when they were drunk or there was a wind and the red flags were flying to show there were dangerous undertows, or they dived into the shallow ends of pools and broke their necks, and they drowned. But Allen had been a friend of Clarke and Clarke had died in a car crash which had officially been listed as accidental, yet which nevertheless had left behind questions which had never been answered . . .

He turned the key and eventually the engine started. He drove through the narrow streets to the square where he was lucky enough to find a parking space near the steps. He walked to the post.

Once seated in his room, he stared at the telephone, his fingers drumming on the desk. Then he made up his mind. He searched through the drawers until he found the handbook of the island's police forces, dialled the telephone number given in this for the guardia post in Repajo—in whose department Playa Turra lay—and asked to speak to someone who could give him details concerning the death of Allen.

A man who spoke with the heavy accent of Galicia said: 'What d'you want to know?'

'Inspector Alvarez, from Llueso . . . Can you give me

the details of the drowning of an Englishman, Simon Allen, off Playa Turra on Monday?'

'There's not much to give, Inspector. He used to go swimming every morning, early. On Monday, he didn't return. His wife got worried and a boat from the harbourmaster's office went out to search.'

'Was it an accidental drowning?'

'There's nothing to say otherwise.'

'Was his body far from shore when it was found?'

'Quite a way. The estimate is half a kilometre.'

'Then there could have been a current which swept him out so far he hadn't the strength to return?'

'At this time of the year with no wind there aren't any currents.'

'Then maybe he hadn't realized how far out he'd gone?'

'His wife says he was a very strong swimmer. He used to go that far out, or farther, every day of the week.'

'Were there any signs of injury?'

'None that I've heard of.'

'Then why'd he drown?'

'Your guess is as good as mine.'

'Is there going to be a PM?'

'I wouldn't think so, unless fresh evidence comes along. Are you saying it might?'

'I just don't know at the moment.'

'So what do I say to the captain?'

'That I'll get in touch if it becomes necessary.'

Alvarez thanked the man, said goodbye, rang off. He leaned back in his chair. A heart attack? (But wouldn't the doctor have been able to judge that that was what killed him — or would it need a PM to determine the question?) Or had he been suddenly stricken by cramp when too far out from the shore to be able to save himself?

It was nearly noon when Alvarez parked his car almost

immediately opposite Tracey's flat. By now the heat was oppressive and it needed considerable will-power to make even the slightest physical effort. Hundreds of people were sunbathing or swimming, more than a dozen yachts were trying to catch the fitful breeze, and two power boats, towing water-skiers, were leaving behind them great white gashes which gradually merged into the travel-poster blue sea.

She was waiting for him on the patio. She was dressed in a bikini which consisted of two scraps of material. 'Hurry up and change.'

'There's something I've got to ask you first . . .'

'You're not asking me anything until we've been swimming. And stop looking at me like that—I'm perfectly decent.'

'Only just!'

'So why are you complaining? Because it's still just?'

'Of course not. You can't think . . .'

She laughed.

It was a long time since he had so enjoyed himself. They swam and they ducked each other and each time his hands touched her body he knew a tingling excitement.

It was nearly two o'clock when they finally returned to her flat.

'Sit down and I'll bring out some drinks,' she said. 'What would you like?'

'A coñac, if you have it.'

'With soda and ice?'

'Just ice, thanks.'

As she went indoors, he closed his eyes and remembered what she'd said the night before. 'How could I be luckier than to die now, when everything's just perfect?' If he died now, everything would be perfect for him . . .

She returned and handed him a glass, then sat. 'Here's to a lot more swims together. Just the one swim has made you shed years.'

'But not enough of them,' he said with sudden sadness.
'Careful, or I'll be reduced to changing your nappies.'
He laughed, to hide his slight sense of shock that she should say such a thing.

She spoke dreamily. 'Wouldn't it be wonderful if we could return to childhood — the nice bits, that is? When it was always sunny and exciting and there was no responsibililty except to wash one's face and hands before a meal. I used to hate washing. I think I really wanted to be a boy. Dad wanted a son, of course, to take on the farm.'

'Is it a big farm?'

'They're very much bigger at home than out here.'

'But is it big in New Zealand?'

'Up to a point,' she answered, with some reluctance.

'Then your parents are rich?'

'Have you ever met a farmer who'll admit to being anything but poverty-stricken?'

'Perhaps you have a big house?'

'I've seen much bigger and more luxurious ones here. You've got to remember, Enrique, that we've pioneer Scottish blood in us. We feel uncomfortable if we're making too much of a show.'

Nevertheless, he imagined a large mansion with richly fertile land stretching all around for as far as the eye could see. He sighed. If he lived away from the tourist areas, having cashed every peseta of his savings, he might, with the help of a generous mortgage from the bank, just be able to afford a small finca with half a dozen hectares of rocky soil, the house of which would be in need of a complete restoration if it were to be lived in by someone who was used to all modern amenities . . .

'Why suddenly so gloomy?'

He lied. 'I was remembering my work and the questions I must ask you.'

'Why the hell have that kind of a memory?'

'I'm sorry.'

'Don't say that. Don't ever be sorry for anything.'

Surprised by her tone, he looked directly at her, but she had turned her face until he could no longer see her expression.

'Well,' she said sharply. 'What questions are so bloody important?'

'Do you remember telling me last night about Simon Allen, who'd drowned? Did you ever meet him?'

'No.'

'Then you knew about him because Señor Clarke had spoken of him?'

'No. And for God's sake, why bring up all this now?'

'I'm . . .'

'You were going to say you were sorry, weren't you?'

'I'm afraid so.'

'If you had . . .' Her tone changed and became lighter. 'I'd have thrown something at you.'

'Then I'm very glad I managed to stop myself.'

She yawned. 'Isn't it funny how tired one gets doing nothing? . . . Drink up and we'll have another before we eat.'

'I wasn't expecting lunch . . .'

'Then aren't you lucky?' She stood. 'Give me your glass.'

He handed it to her and as he did so some trick of sunlight on her flowered bikini momentarily made it seem as if she were wearing nothing.

She left and went inside. Her expression as she'd turned away, he thought, had been quizzical. Had she guessed at the direction in which his imagination had moved? Did a man never learn to control his thoughts until the lid of the coffin was screwed down?

She returned, handed him his glass, sat. 'Why d'you want to know about Simon Allen?'

'His wife says he was a strong swimmer and there were no obvious injuries on his body. So now there's the question of why he drowned?'

'Strong swimmers can drown almost as easily as weak ones because they take much greater risks.'

'That is true. But Señor Clarke died recently in a car crash and it seems strange that two friends should both die in accidents which leave questions.'

'You still think Roger might have been . . . murdered?'

'I just do not know. That is why I ask questions.'

'But why ask them now, when everything was being such fun?'

'I should have waited,' he said contritely.

'Why didn't you?'

He would have done had he not been determined to hide from her the fact that he'd been gloomily imagining the house he might just be able to buy and had been comparing it with the mansion in which she'd lived . . .

'There's something about you which frightens me a little,' she said slowly. 'I'm sure that if you want something you'll go on and on to get it and not stop to count the cost . . . Have you finished asking your beastly questions? Because if you have, I'll get lunch.'

'There's just one more thing. If you never met Señor Allen and Señor Clarke never spoke about him, how did you know they were friends?'

'Because they're together in the photo.'

'What photograph is that?'

She hesitated, then said: 'I've never been someone who tries to keep memories alive: like an aunt of mine who had boxes and boxes full of letters, theatre programmes, scrapbooks, and photographs, and used to look at them by the hour. But after Roger had died and that bitch of his gave me twenty-four hours to clear out of the house, I suddenly felt I needed something to remind me of Roger when we were happy together, right at the beginning and before anything had started to go sour. So I searched for a photo of him. I don't know why, but he's always hated being photographed and I've never owned a camera because I always press the wrong knob, so all I could find was an old photo of him with two other men in it.'

'And one was Señor Allen?'

'That's right.'

'May I see it?'

She went inside, to return almost immediately with a coloured print which she handed to him. Three men, two appreciably younger than the third, stood in a loose group on a beach. In front of one of them was a piece of equipment which, on detailed inspection, he made out to be two scuba tanks in tandem. 'Which one is Señor Clarke?'

She leaned against him, making him very aware of her body, and used her forefinger to indicate the younger man on the right.

'And Señor Allen?'

'He's on the left.'

'Who's that in the centre?'

'I haven't the faintest.'

'Do you know where this was taken?'

'No, I don't, but from the look of things it could easily be somewhere on this island. And I do know that Roger had come out on holidays before he decided to live here.'

He examined the background. There were several tall buildings — tourist-concrete-jungle in style — and behind them mountains, outlined by a deep blue sky. The stark crests of the two tallest mountains, which were next to each other, were bare of pine trees or any visible vegetation and they curved towards each other.

She moved away from him and he was both sorry and relieved that she did so. 'May I borrow this and have a copy made?' he asked.

'Keep it,' she replied.

'But you said you had wanted a memento . . .'

'And now I don't.'

'Are you sure?'

'Damn it, I wouldn't say so if I weren't . . .' Her tone softened. 'Don't look so hurt. You've got to remember it's a woman's privilege to be completely irrational. Come into the kitchen and talk while I get the meal ready. Make me laugh.'

Dolores put her hands on her hips and studied Alvarez with regal displeasure. 'I cooked a special lunch for you.'

'I'm very sorry,' he said humbly. He remembered how Tracey had told him never to apologize. She had not met Dolores.

'I spent all morning in the kitchen.'

Jaime winked at him.

'So what happens?' she demanded rhetorically. 'We wait and wait and in the end the meal is ruined.'

'I got hung up at work.'

'And you could not get word to me, so we could eat before everything was completely ruined?'

'It was rather difficult . . .'

'And in any case, of course, your work was so much more important than any special meal I'd prepared!'

He knew there was only one way in which to try to divert her anger. 'What did you cook?'

'Kidneys in sherry.'

'I'll bet they were really delicious?'

'They were,' she said, disdaining any false modesty and grandly ignoring the fact that only a moment before the meal had been a ruined one.

'I'd have given anything to be able to get back in time. There's no one can do kidneys in sherry like you.'

Jaime picked up a bottle of Soberano. 'Have a coñac?'

Alvarez picked up a tumbler from the table and held it out.

'I know one thing for certain — you'll never be late for a drink,' she said, but her tone was not as sharp as it had

been. She left and went through to the kitchen.
Jaime half filled the tumbler. 'So where were you really?'
'Working.'
'But at what?' Jaime winked again.

CHAPTER 7

Inspector Leyva was a sharply built man with the look of a yappy fox-terrier. He sported a small, tightly clipped moustache and constantly groomed it with the tips of his fingers. He wore unnusually formal clothes even in the height of the summer and his manners—when he was dealing with someone his equal or superior—were inclined to be unctuous rather than very polite.

'I don't understand why you're here,' he said petulantly. Alvarez, he thought, looked as if he'd borrowed someone else's old clothes: his hair had probably not been brushed in days: he had shaved, but badly and there was a thin line of stubble on his left cheek: he had the slack look of a man who drank. When someone like this was a member of the Cuerpo General de Policia, it reflected badly on the whole corps.

Alvarez scratched the back of his neck. 'I'm not certain I know either. The thing is, I've been wondering whether there's any connection between the deaths of Clarke and Allen. Apart from anything else, they knew each other.'

'And that is significant?'

'Well, not on its own, I suppose. But add in the fact that in each case there are unanswered questions . . .'

'Precisely what questions remain unanswered in connection with the death of Señor Allen?'

'As I understand it, he was a strong swimmer and on Monday the sea was calm and there was no wind and virtually no current?'

'Precisely.'

'Then what circumstances caused him to drown? Or to put it in another way, is it quite certain he did die from accidental drowning?'

'The doctor who examined the body, and I quote from memory, reported the classical signs of death by drowning: in particular, a fine froth of inhaled water mixed with mucous was apparent in the mouth. This is entirely symptomatic of the deflation of lungs ballooned by drowning.'

'But was it accidental?'

'He had swum out a long way: perhaps more than half a kilometre.'

'But he was a strong swimmer.'

'However strong, he may have been seized by cramp.'

'What I'm getting at . . .'

'Señor Alvarez, let me interrupt you to say quite categorically that it is my invariable custom to investigate every incident, however minor or straightforward, with the utmost care and attention. I have, therefore, already asked myself whether there were any suspicious circumstances attending his death. And the answer I received was, there are none.'

'Are you asking for a PM?'

'The doctor signed the death certificate immediately after seeing the body and since there was no reason to suspect that death was anything but accidental, the body was released for burial after the obligatory period of waiting. The burial took place last night.'

'I suppose there could be an exhumation.'

'On what grounds?'

'I don't know precisely.'

'This really is going too far! You come here and accuse me of negligence in my work, yet admit you have no facts to support your accusations!'

'Sweet Mary! I'm not accusing you of anything. All I'm

trying to say is that since there was no reason at the time to suspect the death was not accidental, the investigation obviously wouldn't have been quite as thorough as it would have been if you had suspected murder.'

Inspector Leyva spoke coldly. 'Let me say again, I conduct every investigation with the same complete and exhaustive thoroughness, irrespective of the surrounding circumstances.'

'Oh!'

'Had there been the slightest reason for doubt, this death would not have been classified as accidental.'

'I see.' Alvarez paused, then said hesitantly: 'And there were no bruises at all on his body?'

Leyva looked even more annoyed. 'As a matter of fact, the doctor did report very minor bruising on the right ankle.'

'What caused that?'

'It's quite impossible to say. No doubt he banged it on one of the submerged rocks that are close to the shore in the bay.'

'The bruise was caused before death?'

'According to the doctor, yes.'

'You don't think it could be significant?'

'I do not. Now, if you'll excuse me, I am a very busy man.'

'Just one more thing. Would you have any objection to my having a word with the widow?'

Leyva stared at Alvarez and just for a moment it looked as if he were going to smile. 'No objection whatsoever, Inspector. Let me give you the address.'

Vera Allen sat in one of the very luxurious, ugly armchairs in the over-furnished, tastelessly decorated sitting-room. She wore black, but she looked angry and bitter, not desolate—a woman who had been deserted.

'I said at the very beginning I didn't want to come and

live here. Not with everything so dirty. In some of the shops, stuff like flour is in an open sack: what about the mice? And everyone paws the vegetables before they buy what they want. What happens if someone's got something nasty like . . . Well, you know what I mean?'

'Maybe it doesn't matter for the likes of you. You live here and are used to things, but in England our food's wrapped up, like it should be. And what happens when you eat in a restaurant? No tablecloths and the food's covered with garlic so it smells worse'n a Frenchman.'

'Garlic is very good for the health . . .' he began.

'My mother never had any in her house, not in all her seventy-three years. If she could smell what they dish up here and have the nerve to charge for, she'd turn in her grave. And when you're ill, what happens? The doctors can't even speak simple English.'

'Señora, this is Spain . . .'

'I know that all right, don't make any mistake on that score. And I also know what happens when you're ill. I had a pain in the chest and it got so bad I just had to see a doctor. D'you think I could get him to understand what was wrong? Back home even the wog doctors are brighter than him. I could have died for all he understood or cared.'

Alvarez tried to move the conversation along. 'I suppose Señor Allen liked living here?'

'It's different for a man. He can go out on a boat, play golf, or go boozing. What can a woman do?'

'Are there no other English ladies to meet?'

'Them! . . . D'you think they'd ever try to be friendly? Just because I don't sound like the BBC and used to watch *Coronation Street* . . . I wish we'd never left home and come out here to live. Then he'd still be alive.' For a moment, her expression became one of misery, then it changed back to bewildered resentment. 'But he wouldn't take any notice of what I said. Insisted on chucking up his job and coming out here to live and if I didn't like it I could stay at home. Did he think I was going to leave him on his own so he could have fun with every young bitch on the beach?'

'What kind of a job did he have, señora?'

'Worked in the local railway offices. That is, when the lazy sods weren't on strike. I told him, if I went on strike as often as he did, he'd go hungry.'

'Did he have a job here, on the island?'

'You've got to be joking! He told me before we came out that he wasn't going to do another stroke of work for the rest of his life. It's the only time since we got married that he's kept to his word. I'm not lying, if I asked him to pass the paper, he'd tell me to ring for the maid to come and do it.'

'You have a maid?'

'Five days a week and if I worked as little as she does, I'd be ashamed to take the money. Tell her to clean a room and what's she do? Uses a duster to flick the dust from one place to another. She won't use a Hoover. I'm telling you, she just won't use one. Says they're unhygenic: leastways, I think that's what she says. I only took her on because she was supposed to speak English, but if what she speaks is English then I'm a Hottentot. I'd get rid of her only I can't look after a place this size on my own.'

'It looks a very nice house.'

'It's too big and that's what I told Simon when he said he was going to buy it. There's only the two of us and we can't sleep in more than one bedroom at a time, can we? But he always did have big ideas . . .' She stopped and stared into space.

'Was your house in England not so big?'

'Number eight, Oldgate Street? You'd near fit the whole of it into this one room. But the people along the road were friendly and if I wanted a chat all I had to do was walk up and see Gwen or Madge and they'd give me a cup of tea.'

'It must have been quite a change to come out here to live?'

'Ain't that what I've been saying?'

'You were lucky he could give up his job and not have to worry about getting another?'

'Lucky? With him around?'

'I am very sorry. I meant, he must have been left a lot of money.'

'His relatives were all like him. Earn a quid and spend two. There's not one of 'em left anything but debts.'

'But it must have cost a lot to buy this house?'

'That's no lie.'

'Then did he win money in England?'

'He followed the horses, but if he backed one it either retired or came in after the beginning of the next race.'

'Then where did all the money come from, señora?'

'What the hell business of yours is that?'

'I'm sorry, but this is an official investigation and I need to know.'

'Oh, Christ!' She stood. 'I need a drink.'

After she'd left, he visually examined the room again. Together, the furniture and furnishings became garish because they'd been chosen with so little taste, but individually they were of good quality and must have been expensive. The three-piece suite was large and covered in a rich leather, as were the additional matching armchairs: there was an elaborately inlaid desk: the occasional tables were of olive with beautiful graining, such as one seldom saw these days: the bow-fronted display cabinet was filled with intricately carved objects in, probably, ivory: the two large oval carpets were Chinese. The large colour television and video were in a custom-built stand which also housed a large number of tapes. On the other side of the room was a music centre and although he knew little about them, this had the air of being a very good one. A brief and probably very conservative estimate suggested that to buy and furnish this house must have cost around forty million pesetas. Yet before they'd left England, Allen and his wife had lived in a small house and his job could not have been a particularly well paid one.

She returned with two glasses, and without asking him what he wanted, handed him one. She returned to her chair.

'Señora, I regret that I must ask you some more questions.'

She drank. 'Why?' she demanded suddenly and stridently. 'He's dead, isn't he? What's there to question about that?'

'Was he happy living here?'

'He was. Didn't matter to him that I wasn't.'

'Do you know why he decided to live here?'

'Liked it so much when he came out on holiday before we were married. Said the diving was so wonderful because the water was clear. Diving! There's more to life than bloody diving.'

'What kind of diving?'

'With air tanks and a mask. Couldn't stop talking about all the fish he saw. Maybe he thought he was taking over from Jacques Cousteau.'

'I was told he was a very strong swimmer?'

'He had to be good at something apart from drinking, didn't he?'

'Had he been drinking before he went swimming on Monday morning?'

'Give it a break. He was out of the house by half past six. He was a boozer, but he hadn't got round yet to starting that early.'

'And you're quite certain he hadn't complained of feeling ill?'

'He was never ill. Couldn't understand it when I felt like death warmed up.' She finished her drink and stood. 'Let's have your glass for the other half.'

'I haven't finished, thank you.'

'Not like him, are you? Five seconds after you gave him a glass it was empty.'

She left, walking with sufficient care to confirm that this wasn't her first drink of the day. He stared through the nearest picture window. Sad to realize, he thought, that she had had so much and yet enjoyed so little.

She returned.

'Señora, when will you be returning to England?'

'Just as soon as I've sold this place.'

'Is there very much business to decide before you go?'

'I don't know what you're on about?'

'There must be a great deal to arrange with investments and that sort of thing?'

'What investments?' Her voice was now shrill.

'Your husband was quite wealthy. There must be a large amount of capital . . .'

She interrupted him. 'Then suppose you tell me where the hell it is?'

'But there must be some records?'

'When they came and told me he was dead . . .' She drank so eagerly that some of the brandy slopped over her chin. She brushed it away with a finger. 'I went through his papers to see how much money there was. And d'you know how much? By the time I've finished paying funeral expenses and death duties there won't be anything but what this place fetches.'

'Señora, that's impossible. Did you never ask him how you could both afford to come out here and live in such luxury?'

'I did once and he told me to mind my own business. He could get rough so I left it. Besides, it's not a woman's job to know about that sort of thing.'

He remembered Tracey telling him how Clarke had become angry when she'd questioned him about the past.

'Did you ever meet Roger Clarke?'

'Who?'

'Señor Roger Clarke. He lived at Bahia Mocamba.'

'Never heard of him.'

'The señor didn't mention him?'

She made no answer, but finished her drink and then looked across. 'Are you ready now for another?'

'No, thank you, señora. I must drive back home to Llueso.'

Walking still more carefully, though with less success than before, she left the room.

He stood. She'd continue to drink until eventually she found a temporary forgetfulness. A dislikable woman, yet he felt sorry for her.

When she returned she asked him again whether he'd like another drink and on his refusing she became abusive. He interrupted her to say he was leaving and she began to complain stridently that the natives were all the same, completely unfriendly.

Out in the hall he came to a stop, turned, and said: 'Señora, did your husband ever leave this island?'

She drank, caught her breath, coughed, drank again. 'Did he?'

'I couldn't get him to go back home to see everyone. But they were our friends.'

He said quietly: 'Thank you for your kindness.' He hesitated, then added: 'I know it cannot seem so now, but time will help to heal the pain.'

She stared at him. 'Heal the pain?' Her face crumpled and suddenly she was crying. 'How bloody stupid can you get?' she shouted wildly. 'Heal the pain, knowing he'd a woman somewhere and it must be that bitch who's got all his money?'

'Can you give me her name?'

'If I could, I'd have got hold of her and taught her a thing or two.'

'Where does she live?'

'I don't know. When I asked him where he was going, he wouldn't tell me. When I accused him of going to see another woman, he just laughed.' Now, she was sobbing heavily. 'I tell you, he laughed in my face.'

'He saw a lot of her?'

She shook her head.

'How often?' he persisted, hating himself for continuing to question her at such a moment.

'Every year we were here,' she mumbled between sobs.

'Are you saying he only went away once a year.'

'Wasn't that enough for her to get all his money?'

'But if he really was seeing a woman, señora, wouldn't he have visited her much more often?'

She turned and made her unsteady way back into the sitting-room.

He left the house.

CHAPTER 8

Alvarez lay on his bed but for once sleep would not come. The trouble was, his mind kept going round in circles.

Were the two deaths connected or was it just a chain of circumstances which appeared to link them together? He tried to remember all the facts common to Clarke and Allen even when such facts on the face of things could hardly be of any relevancy. Both were approximately of the same age. Both had left England to come to live on the island at approximately the same time. They'd known each other, yet had never admitted to this. Both had bought expensive houses and lived at a luxurious level, although Allen had not been wealthy back in England. (It wasn't clear what Clarke's financial position had been.) After their deaths, there were no signs of the considerable capital that would have been needed to provide them with the income they had clearly enjoyed. Both had resented being questioned about the past. Each had made one or more trips abroad and had refused to take wife or girlfriend along . . .

Alvarez yawned as he suddenly felt sleepy. He looked at his watch. Four-thirty. Perversely, it was now nearly time to get up and return to work. Perhaps, he assured himself, the morning had been so busy and emotionally exhausting that he could allow himself just a few more moments of much needed rest . . . Soon, he was snoring.

Alvarez parked his car and crossed the pavement to enter the frozen food shop. Large freezer units were ranged against the walls and he crossed to the one which contained cuttlefish, spider crabs, crayfish, and many different grades of prawns. The store owner, a short, rotund, cheerful-looking man, came up. 'Enrique! How's life treating you?'

'Very seldom.'

'You're a mournful old bastard, and no mistake.'

'Are those prawns any good?' Alvarez pointed at a box which contained the largest size.

'A king's ransom couldn't buy better.'

'I haven't got a king's ransom. How much are they?'

'Two thousand a kilo.'

'I'm not a foreigner. What's their real price?'

'That's it. Look, I'm not responsible for the prices. It's the government. I'm making so little profit it hurts to think about it. I have to pay eighteen hundred for them: eighteen hundred!'

'Sure. For two kilos.'

The owner always became annoyed when he was accused of profiteering: it was honest hard work which had brought him a house, a finca, three flats let to foreigners, two cars, and a large power boat. 'You know your trouble? You reckon everyone's a liar.'

'That's because of experience.'

The owner pushed the box of very large red prawns to one side and pointed to another of much smaller, pink ones. 'They're only eight hundred.'

'That's hardly surprising . . . What are you going to charge me for half a kilo of the big ones.'

'A thousand, of course.'

'I thought maybe you'd knock a little off?'

The owner was about to disagree when he stopped to consider certain facts. He was in the middle of renovating and enlarging the finca and he hadn't bothered to seek building permission from the town hall: he had, of course, made a tax return for the past year, but because his wife was becoming very extravagant he'd decided to declare only a third of his true income instead of the usual half: he hadn't paid tax on his second car because his cousin worked at the town hall . . . He spoke with sudden bonhomie. 'My dad knew your dad, Enrique, and they were good friends. So for old times' sake, I'll make it nine hundred.'

'Nine hundred for half a kilo? If things keep on like this we'll all have to go back to farming.'

The owner, certain the reference to the country had not been without special significance, kicked the base of the deep-freeze. 'Eight hundred.'

'Seven hundred and fifty.'

The owner picked up the box and carried it over to the small counter on which the scales stood. Two handfuls of prawns weighed five hundred and seventy-five grammes. He went to remove some of the prawns.

'That's all right,' said Alvarez cheerfully.

He returned to the car and drove down to the front and along to Tracey's flat. She was wearing a bikini top and jeans and had been listening to the radio. She switched this off. 'The news is nothing but trouble and it's put me in a down mood. What are you going to do about that?'

'Cook the supper I promised.' He opened the plastic bag and showed her the prawns.

'My God! They're almost like baby lobsters. What are you going to need for the cooking?'

'Olive oil, parsley, garlic, and a lemon.'

'I've everything but the parsley so at some stage I'll have to slip down to Margarita's and buy a bunch. But first, we're going for a voyage so while I put these in the fridge, you change into a costume.'

'A voyage?'

'You're taking me out on a pedallo to the horizon.'

'The horizon? You'll be lucky if I do not collapse before we reach the end of the harbour.'

She put out her hand and rested it on his forearm, in what for him had already become a familiar gesture. 'Stop selling yourself short,' she said, almost angrily. 'You're pefectly strong enough to pedal us both to Shangri-la.'

After the meal they sat out on the patio. The gentle breeze, which had started at dusk, prevented the heat being oppressive and it was another cloudless night with the moonlight strong enough for them to be able to see each other clearly.

He sipped a brandy and listened to her talking about New Zealand and he wondered, sadly, if perhaps her criticism of the lives her parents and sister led was a defence against homesickness . . .

'You're not listening to a word I'm saying.'

He started. 'I'm sorry . . .'

'Didn't I tell you never to say that?'

'Yes, you did.'

'What were you thinking about?'

'As a matter of fact . . .' He stopped.

'As a matter of fact . . .' she mimicked.

'I was wondering about Señor Clarke.'

'Goddamn it, I could kick you where it really hurts! You're sitting here, with me, looking at a romantic bay, and all you can think about is Roger.'

'It's my work.'

'We're supposed to be playing now.'

'You must understand, Tracey. At work I keep asking myself questions and because I'm not clever, the answers refuse to come. And later the questions keep returning to mock me . . .'

She laughed. 'My God, you sound like someone out of a gothic mystery.'

He was sufficiently encouraged by her laughter to ask, diffidently: 'Would you talk a little about him? Then perhaps the questions will go away.'

'Anything for peace, I suppose. But let's have another drink first.'

He refilled their glasses. 'Tracey, did he ever talk about his life before he came to this island?'

'Hardly ever. He was a secretive kind of a guy. But that didn't worry me because I suppose in many ways I'm a secretive kind of a woman. Not that I expect you to believe that!'

'He never mentioned what happened?'

'Just very occasionally he'd let something slip. Like that he went to Oundle.'

'What does that mean?'

'Oundle's one of the big public schools in England.'

'So he came from a big family?'

'He was from an old family, if that's what you're geting at. You know the kind of thing the English go in for— ancestors who were too lucky to be found out and hanged, lots of land and peasants to touch their forelocks, and an overwhelming sense of their divine superiority. But from what he said another time, things had changed more than somewhat. The family had to scrape like hell to pay his school fees. And I don't know what sort of work Roger started at, but when he got married he was obviously not much more than a glorified clerk. He said that his bitch of a wife was always going on at him because he didn't make enough money for them to lead any kind of a social life.'

'Then if he was not wealthy, how was he able to come here and buy a luxurious home and not have to work?'

'Search me.'

'He never gave even a hint?'

'If he did, I wasn't sufficiently interested to pick it up. Just as I'm not now. The subject's boring me and if we don't hurry up and talk about something else I'll develop a nasty headache. You may think you've seen me in a foul temper, but you haven't until you've seen me with a nasty headache.'

On Saturday morning Alvarez entered his office and looked at the telephone on his desk, then went over to the window and stared out at the street below. Forget it, he told himself. He was seeing shadows where there was none. Why be a fool and antagonize Salas by propounding a theory which was, as yet, quite incapable of verification . . . Yet only a little imagination was needed to bond together some of the proven facts . . .

He made up his mind. He would ask Salas to get in touch with England.

He sat at his desk, leaned over, and pulled open the bottom right-hand drawer to bring out the bottle of brandy and a glass. Dutch courage was preferable to no courage at all.

CHAPTER 9

England telexed Palma on Monday morning and Salas immediately telephoned Alvarez. 'The report reads: "Neither Roger Clarke nor Simon Allen has criminal record. Nothing known about either." That is the end of the message.'
'Oh!' said Alvarez, deeply disappointed.
'That is hardly the reply you led me to expect.'
'No, I suppose it isn't.'
'It is extraordinary the ability you have to complicate even the most straightforward and simple events.'
'But it did seem as if the only feasible explanation was that the two men had been involved in some form of criminal activity . . . And if they weren't, where did all the money come from?'
'Is it not a trifle naïve to overlook the fact that no man with any sense declares all he possesses either to his wife or his tax inspector?'
'So far as I can understand, señor, they do things differently in England. And in any case, neither of them had the kind of job where they'd make large sums of money that needed hiding.'
'Nevertheless, wherever the money did come from, it clearly was not from a criminal source. Therefore it does not concern us.'
'Not directly, no. But if I'm right as to the rest of what I said . . .'
'Frankly, that is a presumption I am not prepared to make.'
'Señor, more than ever I have a feeling . . .'
'I am tempted to suggest that the most helpful thing for

you to do will be to take two stomach tablets,' snapped Salas, before replacing the receiver.

Alvarez walked up the road, turned into the square, and crossed to the Club Llueso where he entered the bar. 'A coffee cortado and a coñac.'

'You look as if you'd forgotten to hand in the winning football pool coupon,' said the barman.

'No. It's just work.'

'It's not like you to worry over that.'

'I'm getting old.'

'It happens.' The barman moved away to the espresso machine.

Alvarez sat and stared out through the window at those people at café tables who were visible to him. Foreigners with too much time and money: foreigners who died and in dying made a simple inspector's life hell.

If there were a connection between Clarke and Allen, beyond the known one that they were acquaintances, then the odds increased against their deaths being accidents. And the more one studied the facts, the more difficult it became not to believe that there had been a connection between them. How could wealth come so suddenly? There were three possibilities. Through an inheritance, winning it on some form of gambling, or through a criminal activity. Surely, if they had been left money or had won it, they would have invested at least part of it so that now there would be some record of it? That left some criminal activity which would explain why the money had had to be kept hidden—so well hidden that there was no trace of it. Yet England had negated the possibility that either of them had been engaged in a criminal activity while in the UK.

'Here you are,' the barman called out.

He left the table and went over to the bar.

'A hundred pesetas.'

'Don't you mean ninety?'

'Prices have just gone up on account of the new tax.'

Gloomily Alvarez returned to the table. He sipped the brandy, added sugar to the coffee and drank some of it, then poured the rest of the brandy into the cup. There *had* to be a connection between the two deaths. Despite Superior Chief Salas's scorn, there were times when one had a gut feeling about a case that was taller and broader than logic and could not be denied. But unless fresh evidence came to light there now seemed little chance of ever finding out what that connection was or what part it had played in their deaths.

He shrugged his shoulders. The dead men had been foreigners. He drank the coffee and it warmed his stomach and soothed away his frustrations.

The trawler yacht was an off-shore cruiser, sufficiently seaworthy for quite heavy weather. She was 38 feet long and had, at cruising speed, a range of 1,000 miles or a maximum speed of 20 knots. She possessed a stateroom, a double berth cabin, two toilets and a shower room, a main saloon with dining area, and a deck-level galley. In daylight her lines were more purposeful than beautiful, because of her deep bulwarks and large wheelhouse. But riding to anchor in moonlight, with her lines softened and slightly blurred, she became touched by the sea's romance.

There was virtually no tide and, in that part of the bay where she lay, very little current. She headed south-east while a schooner, moored only a couple of hundred metres away, headed south-west: with her higher superstructure, she was more influenced by the breeze. A light shone from her saloon and this, shimmering, stretched across the water almost parallel to the moonlight's path. Beyond that, there were no signs of life aboard her.

At 2304 hours — the time was logged by the assistant

harbourmaster—there was a heavy explosion and seconds later flames belched out of her shattered accommodation. The assistant harbourmaster called on the crew of a fishing-boat, about to put to sea, to help him and they sailed him over to the blazing vessel. Showing considerable courage, he tried to quell the fire with the two chemical extinguishers he'd taken with him, but it proved a hopeless task.

The boat continued to burn until sufficient of the hull had been consumed for the sea to enter. She began to settle, the flames retreated, and finally she sank. As she went down, a badly burned body floated clear of her. Overcoming the nausea which the task produced, the assistant harbourmaster lashed the body to the side of the fishing-boat and then gave orders for them to return to the harbour.

CHAPTER 10

On Tuesday morning, Alvarez parked by the side of the harbourmaster's office, half way up the eastern arm of the harbour, and went inside. The harbourmaster, a grizzled man in his late fifties, shook hands. 'Well, we've identified him, Enrique. We'd the name of the boat from when she arrived—*Janet II*—and I've checked her out. She was from Palma, on charter, and the man who chartered her was called Peter Short.'

'Was he English?'

'That's right.'

'Here on holiday?'

'That's not clear. But apparently he owns a house just outside Llueso, so he may live here. He told the charterers that a friend of his was coming over from England and he wanted to take him to Menorca.'

'Did they have any idea when the friend's supposed to arrive?'

'I didn't bother to ask.'

'Did the charterers give you his address?'

The harbourmaster looked down at a sheet of paper on his overcrowded desk. 'Ca Na Rostra. They think he told them it was up the Laraix valley.'

'Have you any idea what caused the explosion?'

'Can't be certain, of course, but I'll give you ten to one it was leaking gas. All the boats these days have bottled gas for the cookers and refrigerators and the equipment isn't always maintained as it should be — they don't renew the tubing every third year: that sort of thing. The gas escapes and as it's heavier than air it sinks to the deck and gradually builds up. Something causes a spark and . . .' He clicked his thumb against his middle finger.

'Later on, I'll want a word with the charterers — who are they?'

'Bonnin. They're a big firm and their boats are usually good. So don't expect them to admit that any of the gas lines or equipment could have been faulty.'

Laraix valley stretched from Llueso to the Sierra de Roig which were part of the chain of mountains which, running from east to west, formed the backbone of the island. At no point wider than a kilometre, with stark mountains to the west and smaller, more civilized hills to the east, the valley in summer had a rugged beauty: in winter, however, when clouds stretched from side to side to enclose it, it became a dour, unfriendly, and at times even menacing place.

Ca Na Rostra was along a dirt track which led off the single metalled road. Set in an oblong field in which grew oranges, lemons, grapefruit, walnuts, almonds, pomegranates, and figs, the stone-built, two-hundred-year-old house had been heavily and unsympathetically restored.

Originally box-shaped, arched balconies and flat-roofed extensions had turned it into a surburban folly: the folly was compounded by a kidney-shaped swimming pool with changing rooms and barbecue area in Roman style beyond.

Alvarez knocked on the front door. A wheeling raptor above the field was working a thermal while not far below it a flight of pigeons passed, unconcerned: the shrilling of cicadas was constant: in the next field, the bells around the necks of a flock of sheep maintained an unmusical, but not offensive, jangling: from a distance came the high pitched, unvarying note of an engine working a water-pump. There was no answer to his knock. He used a handkerchief to wipe the sweat from his face and neck, then tried the door to find it locked. He walked round the side of the house to the back door which was half wood, half glass, and tried that: it also was locked and in none of the obvious hiding places was there a key.

He returned to his car and drove up the long, loose-surfaced drive to the dirt track, turned left, and then stopped when level with a small house on the right-hand side. An elderly man was watering a flower-bed with a hose. Alvarez climbed out of the car. 'Good morning, señor,' he said in English, taking note of the floppy sun hat, the white shirt with slightly frayed collar, baggy shorts, socks, plimsolls, and tight moustache.

''Morning,' replied the Englishman in clipped tones which made it clear he was not buying anything.

Alvarez introduced himself.

'And my name's Barker . . . You've come about the break-in at the Attrays', have you? As it happened only a couple of weeks ago, I suppose you're really on the ball!' He gave a short, sharp bark of sound which might have been a laugh.

'No, señor, I regret I have not come about that.' The name of Attray seemed vaguely familiar, he thought.

Perhaps it appeared in one of the reports lying about his desk. 'I would like to speak about Señor Short, who owns the house down there.'

'That's more than I would.'

'You do know him?'

'Depends what you mean by know. I've met the fellow. But I've taken damn good care not to get to know him . . . Blast!' He had not been concentrating on what he'd been doing and in consequence had kept the hose directed at one spot for too long with the inevitable consequence that the crumbly soil had begun to wash away. 'Here, hold this while I go and turn off. And watch where you point it.' He left, disappearing round the corner of the house.

Alvarez took the hose and almost immediately he saw, to his horror, a couple of Sweet William plants washed out of the ground. He hurriedly put the hose down on the lawn of gama-grass, knelt, and forced the plants back into the soil with scant regard for their root systems. His shoe hit the hosepipe and the nozzle swung round to soak his knees before the flow stopped. He had only just regained his feet when Barker returned.

'Soaked yourself, I see. You Mallorquins don't know the first thing about gardening. The wife went into the local gardening centre the other day and found 'em selling nemophila as poppies. And when she pointed that out, damned if the assistant didn't just shrug his shoulders and say they looked alike so it didn't matter . . . Here, give me the hose before you smash that up somehow. You want a drink, I suppose?'

'Thank you very much, señor.' Alvarez handed over the hose.

'Never known one of you chaps to say no.' His complexion suggested that neither did he say no very often.

On the south side of the house there was a small patio, with overhead vine, on which were set out a table and four chairs, made from metal and showing signs of rust.

'Grab a seat,' said Barker. 'Now, what'll it be? There's no whisky because I can't afford it and gin's a woman's drink. So you can have brandy, rum, or beer, or some of that bloody awful sweet vermouth muck my wife has.'

'I would like a coñac, please.'

'You mean a brandy. Cognac comes from Cognac. Ice and soda?'

'Just ice, please.'

Barker went inside the house and Alvarez tried to find an easier sitting position in a chair whose elaborate wrought-iron back seemed designed for discomfort.

Barker returned with two tumblers, each three-quarters filled, and handed one across before he sat. 'The wife's shopping. She's always shopping. Women's disease.' He drank, put the glass down on the table, brushed his moustache with crooked forefinger. 'So what d'you want to know about the fella, Short?'

'You may not have heard, but sadly he died last night.'

'Really?'

'You do not sound very distressed?'

'I'm not a man to start addressing the angels the moment someone dies. He was a rotter. Always trying to suck up to the wife.' He snorted. 'She put him in his place and no mistake!'

'What kind of rotter was he?'

'There aren't different kinds. One is or one isn't.'

'Was he wealthy?'

'He paid eight million for the house and that was before prices soared. Bloody fool. Have you seen it?'

'Only from the outside.'

'Like a babu brothel.'

'D'you know when he bought it?'

Barker thought for a moment. 'Must be something like three years ago.'

'Did he live there?'

'No, thank God!, or we'd have had him around more

often since he was too thick-skinned to understand. He came here on holiday.'

'Then he lived in England?'

'Somewhere on the Continent. Never said where and I'm damned if I ever cared. He'll have been on the tax fiddle lark — his kind always are.'

'Was he married?'

'How the devil would I know that?'

'He never had his wife here when he was on holiday?'

'Never seen him with a woman. Not that he'll have been able to keep away from the tarts.'

'Does he employ a maid?'

'There's a woman who looks after the place all the year round: keeps it clean and aired, that sort of thing.'

'Do you know her name?'

'Don't know anything about her except she moves around on one of those motorized bikes. Damned dangerous machines . . . Here, what's the matter?'

'Matter with what, señor?'

'You're not drinking. Damnit, it's perfectly good brandy.'

'Indeed, it is. It's just that I was thinking.'

'Leave that to other people. You'll lead a happier life that way.'

On his return to the office, Alvarez telephoned home. 'It's me,' he said, when Dolores answered. 'Do you know who works for Señor Short, an Englishman who lives in Ca Na Rostra, which is up the Laraix valley?'

She thought for a moment, then said: 'I'm not certain, Enrique. I don't think Ana goes there and Carolina hasn't any work at the moment. Julia is in the port and so's Rosalía . . .'

He interrupted her before she detailed every one of her friends. 'Can you try and find out?'

'Yes, all right. Why d'you want to know?'

'The señor sadly died last night in an explosion aboard a boat at anchor in the bay.'

'Mother of God!' she exclaimed.

After he'd rung off, he leaned back in his chair and stared at the window, still shuttered so that the room was in half light. At this stage, any connection with the deaths of Clarke and Allen — and were they connected? — was obviously tenuous in the extreme. Short had been wealthy, he'd bought his house about three years previously, he'd lived outside England, and he'd died in what appeared to have been an accident. Yet what were the odds against even these few similarities occurring in three deaths over so relatively short a period? . . . Had Short known Clarke and Allen? What had his circumstances been back in England? Had he visited the island before he'd bought the house?

The new morgue had been built by the side of one of the two firms of undertakers in Llueso. Many of the villagers crossed themselves as they walked past it and even the children regarded it with a certain awe. Inside, there was a small reception area, an office, a cloakroom, and the main room with cold storage shelves.

The man who looked after the morgue was squat, hairy, and cheerful, and quite unperturbed by the fact that he was generally known as Marcelo the Dead.

'He's a bit messed up,' he said.

'I didn't expect him to be covered in roses,' replied Alvarez, who hated the morgue and everything to do with it.

Marcelo pulled out one of the refrigerated shelves which, despite its weight, rolled easily on runners set on ball-bearings. There was a light green rubber sheet and he drew this back.

The body had been so extensively burned that, ironically, the horror was less than if its appearance had been more normal. Due to the contraction of muscles from heat, the posture was the typical pugilistic attitude — clenched fists on bent arms.

'Are there any special identifying physical features?' Alvarez asked.

'There's been no call to check. But you're not going to find out much this side of a PM, are you? . . . The only thing I've noticed is the ring on his right hand.'

Alvarez moved down the side of the shelf until he could examine the hand. The ring was blackened, but had not begun to melt. There was some form of signet, but it would be impossible to make out exactly what this was until the ring was cleaned. 'I wonder if they'll be able to get his prints?'

'When he's burned this hard?'

'It's amazing what they can do these days. They get the imprint from under the surface skin.'

'What d'you want 'em for?'

'He's not going to be positively identified any other way, is he?'

'Don't you know who he is, then?'

'Sure. But my boss is one of those people who wants everything treble-checked.'

'The world's full of stupid bastards,' said Marcelo philosophically.

The bush telegraph in Llueso operated with enviable efficiency. Although about ten thousand people lived in the village, by the time Alvarez returned home for lunch, Dolores had discovered the name of the woman who worked at Ca Na Rostra.

Juana Ortiz had been widowed over two years ago, but in the face of a rapidly changing custom, she still wore black. She was good-looking, though on the plump side, and might easily have married again had she not held to the traditional view that a widower might remarry, but a widow might not. She worked in order to support her daughter at Barcelona University: her son was doing his military training.

Alvarez knew her, if not well, and for a while their conversation concerned her children, but then he said: 'I expect you've heard about Señor Short?'

She nodded.

'Will it distress you to answer a few questions about him?'

She fidgeted with a button on her black cotton dress. 'The Lord rest his soul, but he was not a very nice man,' she said, by way of an oblique answer.

'When did you last see him?'

'It was only yesterday.'

'How was he?'

'It's difficult to say. I mean, he didn't know any Spanish and I know little English, so we couldn't really talk to each other.'

'How long had he been here this visit?'

She thought. 'It must have been about ten days.'

'D'you know where he'd come from?'

She shook her head. As for so many of the islanders, the world beyond was, despite TV, virtually unknown and she had very little interest in it.

'Did he ever talk about England?'

'But I've just said, we couldn't really understand each other.'

'I wondered if perhaps you'd picked up something?'

'No, nothing.'

'Was he married?'

'I've never seen a woman in the house.'

'How often did he come out to the island?'

'Maybe two or three times a year.'

'Did you know that yesterday he was meeting a friend who was coming over from England?'

'He did say something about it.'

'Any idea what his friend's name was?'
'No. I'm sorry, Enrique, but . . .' She shrugged her shoulders.
'Don't worry, you're doing fine. Is there anything you can tell me about his friend? When did he arrive?'
'I know nothing except the señor told me he had to be at the airport by a quarter past six in the evening . . . At least, I think that's what he was saying. He used to get so annoyed when I couldn't understand him.'
'The friend wasn't staying at Ca Na Rostra?'
'I don't think he can have been. I mean, the señor didn't ask me to get one of the spare bedrooms ready, which I could have done easily as the house was as clean as a new pin from top to bottom. Sweet Mary! he had me dusting, wiping down, and washing, as if the Queen were coming to stay.'
'Did he keep his papers anywhere about the house — business files, that sort of thing?'
'I've never seen any around, but there's a safe in the wall of one of the downstairs rooms so perhaps there are some there.'
'Where's the key of the safe?'
'How would I know a thing like that?'
'But you'll have a key to the house?'
'Yes, of course.'
'Will you let me have it, please?'
She left the room and when she returned she handed him two keys, one a Yale type and the other of regular pattern. 'They're both for the back door. You will take care of them, won't you?'
'Of course,' he assured her.
'What shall I do about cleaning the house tomorrow?'
'I think that for the moment you'd better stay away. I'll let you know what's happening when I bring the keys back.'
She hesitated, then said: 'Some French people who've come to live in the village asked me to work for them, but

I said I didn't have the time. But with the señor gone, perhaps the next people to live in the house won't want me . . . ?'

'If you want my advice, go back to the French people and say you're free after all.'

She nodded.

He pocketed the keys. He had, he thought, learned nothing of any consequence — which was to say, nothing which connected Short's death with those of Clarke and Allen.

CHAPTER 11

Alvarez unlocked the back door of Ca Na Rostra and went inside. The kitchen, an extension built on to the north side of the house, was large and very well equipped: washing-up machine, microwave oven as well as a split-level gas oven, two kinds of mixers, an American refrigerator with a crushed ice dispenser, a cabinet deep-freeze, and a water-softener. Money, and plenty of it.

He passed through to the passage which gave access to a small room that was obviously a study, the dining-room and, beyond that, the sitting-room. He returned to the study. It was less than half the size of the kitchen and was made smaller by the large desk. To the right of the bookcase was a coloured print of a square-rigger under full sail and behind this was a safe. He checked the drawers of the desk but the key of the safe was not in any of them, then went over to the small glass-fronted cupboard, opposite the bookcase, but the key wasn't in that. Yet so many people, ignoring all the canons of security, kept the key of a safe as close as possible to it, fondly believing that no intruder would ever think of searching for it. Under the carpet? He found it under the corner farthest from the door.

Inside the safe there were no papers, only a number of five-thousand-peseta notes. He counted them. Ninety-two. Four hundred and sixty thousand pesetas. A lot of money to have in cash, by most people's standards.

He returned the money, locked the safe, and put the key back under the carpet. Then he sat on the corner of the desk. Was there more significance in what he hadn't found than in what he had? No cheque-books, no travellers' cheques, no passport. (They might have been on the boat.) No personal papers of any sort and in particular no copy of a will. Nothing, in fact, that would begin to lift up a corner of his life. So was he a man who had drawn an iron curtain between the past and himself, as Clarke and Allen had tried to do?

Alvarez left the study and went upstairs. There were four bedrooms, each with an en suite bathroom: one of these was slightly larger than the others and it was the only one in which either of the twin beds was made up. Built-in cupboards stretched the length of one wall and in one of these, taking up only a small part of the available space, were a lightweight suit, two pairs of trousers, underwear, four casual shirts and one formal one, socks, a lightweight sweater, and three pairs of shoes. In the pockets of the suit and trousers there was only money — four thousand pesetas in the suit, two thousand in the hip pocket of one pair of trousers, and three thousand in the right-hand pocket of the other pair.

He returned downstairs to the sitting-room. On one of the occasional tables was a silver tray on which were two bottles and two glasses. He went over to the settee and sat. How was he going to start uncovering the dead man's background? Hopeless to get in touch with England and ask them for information concerning a Peter Short, address unknown but not in Britain, background not known . . .

He suddenly remembered. The friend Short had told

Juana he was meeting at the airport. He'd had to be there by six-fifteen. Presumably that was roughly the time of arrival of the plane. Palma airport was one of the busiest in Europe in the summer, but with that information it might be possible to work out which plane he'd been meeting . . . And he'd shown his passport to the charterers of the boat who would have noted the number for their records . . .

'Enrique,' Tracey said, with careful restraint, 'I know nothing in this country ever starts on time except a bullfight, but do you really have to be an hour and a half late?'

'I'm sorry, but I've been so busy . . .'

'Stop saying you're sorry. And, goddamn it, I've been even busier, trying to keep my temper.'

'Unfortunately, without success.'

She stared at him, then suddenly laughed. 'Tell me something interesting. Why is it I can never get really angry with you?'

'That's not correct. The other day . . .'

'I said, really angry. The other day I was just beginning to become annoyed.' She tucked her arm round his and started across the patio towards the front door of her flat. 'Never mind, all that really matters is that you've finally made it. The brandy bottle's ready, the ice bucket is full, your costume's hanging in the bathroom, and there's a special surprise for supper.'

Welcome home, he thought.

On Wednesday morning Alvarez arrived at the guardia post at eight thirty-three.

'Good grief!' exclaimed the duty guard, 'it's only just daybreak. Has the revolution broken out?'

Alvarez went up to his room and settled behind the desk. He brought out a telephone directory from one of the drawers, checked the number of Palma airport, and dialled it. Unusually, the call was answered after no more than a dozen rings.

'I want to talk to someone about incoming flights last Monday evening,' he said.

'There's no one here,' replied the woman at the other end, faithfully observing the first principle of airport authorities that the general public should be denied all possible information.

'Cuerpo general de Policia.'

'Oh!' she said angrily. 'Then I suppose you'll have to have a word with Traffic. Hang on.'

The line clicked and buzzed, there was a transitory and tantalizing snatch of conversation between two ladies, and then a man said: 'Yes?'

He explained what he wanted.

The man spoke wearily. 'I suppose you realize that at this time of the year aircraft are arriving every few minutes?'

'Yes, I do.'

'So therefore it could take one hell of a long time to work out what you want to know.'

'That's all right. I'm not particularly rushed.'

'I wasn't thinking of you . . . All right, give me your number and we'll get on to you when we know something.'

Despite the man's pessimism, he rang back three-quarters of an hour later. 'Within those times you gave me, planes came in from Edinburgh, London Gatwick, London Heathrow, Stockholm, Zürich, Frankfurt, Marseilles, Lyons, Madrid and Barcelona.'

'Can you give me the airlines of the planes from the UK?'

'Hang on a sec.'

He waited.

'Heathrow was Iberia, Edinburgh was British

Caledonian, and Gatwick was UK Tours.'

'You wouldn't also know which travel firms were working those flights?'

'I would not.'

After ringing off, Alvarez picked up a pencil from his paper-strewn desk and fiddled with it, but try as he might he could think of no short cut for what had to be done next. Sighing, he telephoned each of the three airline companies in turn and asked for a list of the travel firms who had been working those flights. His request was met with annoyance which shaded into anger, but by a judicious mixture of flattery and authority he finally persuaded each of the companies to check their records for him.

He telephoned the four solicitors who practised in Llueso and the fourth one said that he had handled the legal work connected with the purchase of Ca Na Rostra.

'Do you know if Señor Short made a will?'

'I advised him it was necessary because of the danger of dying intestate, but he said he'd get around to it later. I couldn't do more.'

'So as far as you know, he's died intestate?'

'Unless, of course, he made a will through someone else.'

'I'll have to get on to Madrid to check. Tell me, when you were handling the matter, did you ever learn anything about him? Whether he was married, where he'd lived in Britain, and where he was living in Europe?'

'I don't think so, although it's all some time ago now. As I remember him, he was one of those men who never says any more than's absolutely necessary.'

'How did he pay for the house?'

'I'd have to look in my records to answer that.'

'Will you do it?'

'It could take a bit of time so I'd better ring you back.'

Alvarez replaced the receiver. Now, he was going to

have to telephone each of the different banks to see if Short had an account at any of them and it sometimes seemed as if there were more banks on the island than bureaucratic offices . . . Nevertheless, he could confirm some time later that not one of the banks on the island held, or had ever held, an account in the name of Peter Short.

The solicitor rang back. 'I managed to find out what you wanted to know, although it's taken all this time. Shall I send the bill in to you?'

'Just add something extra to your clients' accounts.'

He chuckled. 'D'you think I've left enough room for that? . . . Señor Short bought Ca Na Rostra for eight million and he paid in cash.'

Alvarez whistled. 'Did that strike you as odd?'

'It's not the first time. When there were currency restrictions in Britain, buyers often paid in cash they'd smuggled out. Nowadays, it's the French. Tomorrow, like as not, it'll be people taking their money back out of Spain.'

Alvarez thanked him and rang off. Immediately, the telephone rang. He stared at the receiver with bitter dislike before lifting it. Iberia gave him a list of four holiday firms. He wrote the names down and began to search through the telephone directory for the numbers of the firms, but British Caledonian interrupted him. They gave him five names. He was sadly contemplating the list and mentally estimating the effort that was going to be involved in contacting each of the nine firms when UK Tours added seven more names. Sixteen calls to make: sixteen people to whom he had to explain what he wanted and then persuade or browbeat into doing it for him . . .

He leaned over and opened the bottom right-hand drawer of the desk and brought out the glass and bottle of brandy.

He did not return to Calle Juan Rives until two-fifteen in the afternoon. The family had just finished their meal.

'You'll have eaten, of course,' said Dolores, very offhandedly.

'I'm blowed if I have. I'm starving,' he replied as he reached across the table for the bottle of red wine.

'I thought you must have done and just couldn't be bothered to let me know.'

'I like that! I've been working flat out until I left the office and came straight back here.'

Jaime sniggered, making it clear that he didn't believe so unlikely a story.

Alvarez did not finish telephoning until twenty past seven in the evening. Exhausted, he stared down at his notes. As was only to be expected, the many tour operators had taken the tourists from the three UK flights to hotels in virtually every part of the island. But, and it did seem as if luck were partially with him since it was reasonable to suppose that Short's friend would be staying in a hotel not too far from Short's house, only one operator had brought tourists to the north-east end of the island. Their courier lived in Playa Nueva and she visited each hotel each day and no doubt would be able to help him. Her name was Señorita Brown.

Caroline Brown was plump and cheerful and, necessary in her job, seldom upset by anything other people said or did. She spoke Spanish fluently, even to the extent of using her hands eloquently.

She and Alvarez sat outside the ugly ten-storey hotel, by the side of a pool in which a number of people were swimming despite the lateness of the hour. From inside the hotel came the beat of disco music and frequently the shouts of guests who had underestimated the potency of the wine.

'Yes, I can tell you who it was,' she said. 'His name's Charles Prade and he's been unlucky and suffered from Franco's fury . . . Oh my God! My mother always told me my tongue was five seconds faster than my brain.'

'Señorita, I can't understand what you're telling me.'

'Well, I . . . I'm sorry. But in the old days, when a client got a case of the trots the courier always used to call it Franco's fury. Rather like Montezuma's revenge. But of course it's not polite and . . . and maybe you . . .' She became silent.

'The trots are what?'

'An upset tummy. People come out and get one and they say it's the water or the oily food, but nine times out of ten it's because they've been drinking too much cheap red wine.'

'How can you be certain it is Señor Prade I wish to speak to?'

She spoke quickly, eager to have her recent *faux pas* forgotten. 'There's nothing clever about it! I was at the airport, as always, to meet the customers. You know what I have to do? The passengers travelling with our firm identify me by my uniform and badge and they come up after passing through Customs and I tell 'em which bus to go to. Sounds easy, but mind you it can be a job and a half because there's always some goon who never reads what to do on arrival and then wanders around like a lost sheep and I go barmy because the numbers aren't right and the bus drivers say they're leaving . . . Anyway, I was doing this and had finished and was going out to the buses when a man came up to me and said he wouldn't be going on a bus after all because his friend had unexpectedly met him and he was returning with the friend and he'd be along to the hotel later in the evening and would that be all right? I told him, now I know what's happening you can take off to where you like.'

'Which hotel's he staying at?'

'The Don Emilio in Cala Bastón. That's on the sea front, at the far end of town. A bit nicer than most of the others and the food's good. I always eat there when I can.'

'When I was a boy,' he said sadly, 'Cala Bastón was just a beach.'

'Then it's changed!' There was no regret in her voice for peace and solitude lost. If the island had not been a Mecca for tourists, she'd be living in Birmingham.

By the time he drove into Puerto Llueso, the front cafés and restaurants were still busy but elsewhere the port had quietened and there was little traffic passing Tracey's flat. He climbed the rickety wooden stairs and reached the outside patio to see that the window shutters were closed and the curtain had been drawn across inside the door. He checked the time: a quarter past eleven. He'd warned her that because of his work he couldn't guarantee when he'd be along and she'd said it didn't matter, he was to come, yet if she were already asleep she'd have every right to be annoyed. On the other hand, she might still be awake, reading, waiting for word from him . . . He decided to compromise and tapped lightly on the door so that if she were asleep he wouldn't wake her. After a moment, the curtain was drawn aside. Tracey unlocked the door. She was wearing a short embroidered nightdress of some filmy material and in the soft light, a mixture of moonlight and diffused street lighting, it had suggestions of transparency.

'I'm very sorry to be so late,' he said formally, trying to keep his gaze on a level with her head, 'but I've only just finished work. I hoped you wouldn't actually have gone to bed.'

'I wasn't asleep because I knew you'd be along when you could . . . Don't keep standing there like a lost soul, come on in.'

'Perhaps . . . perhaps it would be better if I left?'

'When you haven't really arrived? What's the matter? Don't you want to come in?'

He swallowed heavily.

'Enrique,' she murmured, 'you're one goddamn fool. Do I have to put the invitation in writing?'

He stepped inside and she shut the door, locked it, and pulled the curtain across.

CHAPTER 12

Alvarez stood at the kitchen table and dunked the last piece of featherlight ensaimada into the bowl of hot cocoa. Dolores saw him smile and she opened her mouth to speak and then, most uncharacteristically, said nothing. She went over to the cooker, picked up a saucepan, and put this down on the marble working surface with unnecessary force.

As he chewed, he stared out through the open window at the small courtyard and the tangerine tree which was half in sunshine. 'Looks like it's going to be a nice day,' he said enthusiastically.

'What d'you expect at this time of the year?'

He chuckled. 'You sound as if you got out of the wrong side of the bed this morning.'

'And you sound . . .' She stopped.

'How do I sound?'

The word ridiculous tickled her tongue, but she managed to contain it. She picked up the saucepan and returned it to the cooker, banging it down with even more force than before. 'I saw Victoria yesterday.'

'So now I understand why you're fed up with life,' he said gaily, careless of the fact that the two women were from time to time quite friendly.'

Her lips tightened, but before she would say anything more Juan came into the kitchen. She ordered him out in so sharp a voice that he almost ran, his expression both worried and hurt.

Alvarez finally realized that the storm signals were flying. 'I'd better get moving—got a lot to do.' He picked up the bowl and drained the cocoa.

'Victoria told me she saw you the day before yesterday.'

'Yes? Well, I must be off . . .'

'She says you were with a foreign woman. Is it because of this woman that you're always late home?'

'I've told you, I'm having to work myself silly and . . .'

'You were working until five this morning?'

'What d'you mean?'

'I heard you creep in.'

'Well, I . . . I had to go to a hotel over in Ca'n Nestat and I had a drink or two and . . .'

'Enrique, listen to me.' Her tone had changed and now was no longer sharp but pleading. 'For someone like you there can be nothing but sorrow from going out with a foreign woman. You're too . . . too emotional and you don't understand what they have become. For you, love is something sacred: for them, it is something they throw away as easily as a cigarette stub.'

'You don't know her so you're talking nonsense.'

'Is it true that she's much younger than you?'

'What if she is?' he demanded roughly. 'Can't you understand that sometimes age doesn't mean a thing? It's how people feel that matters, not how old they are. Why shouldn't I go out with a foreigner? D'you think we're still living in the times when people crossed themselves if they saw one because they were scared it was the devil in disguise?'

'Don't get angry. I'm trying to help you.'

'You've a very funny way of showing that.'

'I love you too much to stand around and see you being hurt.'

'It's you who's hurting me, not Tracey.'

She stared at him for a few seconds, desperate to find the words that would make him understand, then she turned away, shoulders slumped. The foreigners had brought with them so much money that every islander's life had been changed out of all recognition. But as far as she was concerned, far from being grateful, that was one of the reasons for fearing and disliking them.

Cala Bastón, fifteen kilometres along the coast from Puerto Llueso, was an alien, anonymous place of hotels, apartment blocks, villas, restaurants, shops, discothèques, and topless bars, which existed solely to serve the tourist trade: it owed nothing to the island. Although holiday-makers of many countries did stay there, by far the majority were German and this fact was reflected by the menus printed in German, the rye bread, the variety of lagers, and the memento shops with their carved wooden figures of ample proportions and slightly salacious natures.

The Don Emilio was on the front at the western end of the town and the tall, oblong building, using coloured panels on the outside walls to break up the otherwise stark lines, was set in gardens which were bright and colourful almost all the year round.

The receptionist said Señor Prade was, as far as he knew, still in his room. He telephoned Room 231, then handed the receiver over. Alvarez introduced himself.

Prade, around thirty, just short of six feet tall, a head of straight black hair, rugged rather than handsome, wearing a casual blue shirt and grey cotton trousers, came down the main staircase to the lobby. He shook hands with a firm, dry grip.

'I'm sorry to bother you, señor, when I understand you

are not very well,' said Alvarez.

'How the hell d'you know that?'

'I had a word with Señorita Brown.'

'Did you, then! Nice girl that, and efficient. Got hold of some medicine for me that really did the trick so I'm virtually back to normal.' He grinned sardonically. 'Got to be fit to go back home and tell everyone what a wonderful holiday I've had.'

'Señor, can you have a coffee with me in the television room?'

'I'm up to drinking coffee, yes . . . Look, what's wrong?'

'Please come with me.'

There were no guests in the television room, but a maid was sweeping the floor. Alvarez asked her in Spanish to leave and she looked at them with worried curiosity before going.

Alvarez said: 'I fear I have some serious news which you may not have heard. Sadly, during Monday night Señor Peter Short suffered a serious accident from which he died.'

'My God!'

Alvarez led the way over to one of the tables and sat. Prade brought out a pack of cigarettes and took one, then, with a start, remembered his manners and offered it. 'What kind of an accident?'

'The señor had chartered a boat in Palma and sailed it round to Puerto Llueso, where he moored. He was aboard when there was an explosion which started a fire. It was impossible to put the fire out and the boat sank. His body was recovered.'

'Jesus!' Prade fiddled with his cigarette. 'Even though he wasn't a close friend, it's still one hell of a shock! I mean, when you see someone in the evening and you learn he died that same night . . .'

'Señor, were you not expecting to sail to Menorca with him?'

'You seem to know more about me than I do myself! How d'you learn that?'

'The harbourmaster told me, after he'd spoken to the charterers . . . Were you not surprised when you didn't see him again on the Tuesday?'

'Yes, of course.'

'But you didn't try to get in touch with him to find out what had happened?'

'I was going to, of course, but his name wasn't in the telephone book and one of the desk clerks told me that there are still a lot of houses without the phone. Then I went down with this tummy bug and that made life very difficult. And on top of that . . . I don't know quite how to explain without making myself seem a bit . . . well, precious. When he first suggested taking me for a boat trip I reckoned it was probably because he'd nothing better to do. You know what it's like — a holiday in the sun sounds wonderful, but if you're on your own it can become pretty boring. So when I didn't hear from him again I put it down to the fact that he'd probably found something better to do. And I suppose I'd better admit that I was a bit piqued and wasn't going to go chasing him.'

The door opened and a waiter, carrying a tray, entered. He put the tray down on the table in front of them and left.

They helped themselves to milk and sugar.

'Señor, because of certain facts concerning the death of Señor Short, I have to try and find out more about him. Will you help me do this?'

'Yes, of course. But I must stress that we weren't close friends.'

'I understand. When and where did you first meet him?'

'In Paris, something like eighteen months ago. We were both staying at the Hotel Grimauld — in the Rue

Clément-Marot, I think—and having a drink at the bar. When you're abroad you talk more freely to strangers and we were roughly the same age so we started chatting. We got on quite well together and went out and about a couple of times.'

'Was he on his own?'

'Yes, there was no one with him.'

'Was he on holiday?'

'Not completely. He did talk about having some business to do.'

'Did he mention what kind of business?'

'If he did, I've forgotten.'

'Can you suggest what it might have been?'

'No, beyond the fact that he obviously made a fair bit of money at it.'

'When did you next see him?'

'A couple of months later on. I was in my flat in London and the phone rang and it was him. He suggested dinner together.'

'Where did he live?'

'I never found out. He seemed always to be on the move. As a matter of fact, I did ask him once where his base was, but he very carefully didn't answer.'

'If he had no permanent address, how did you get in contact with him?'

'I didn't. He always got in touch with me.'

'Did you not find this unusual?'

'Yes. But then there was something just a bit odd about him . . . He was good fun, amusing, knowledgeable about a lot of things, but the moment the conversation ever became at all personal, he clammed up. I remember I once asked him where he'd gone to school. He behaved as if I'd just tried to borrow a hundred quid. His secrecy used to irritate me, but I learned to live with it.'

'When did you last see him before you came here?'

'A few weeks ago, in London. We had dinner together

at a Chinese restaurant. I said work was getting me down and I was worn out and ripe for a holiday and that's when he said I ought to have a break out here. He told me he'd hire a boat and sail to Menorca. Incidentally, and just to show you how secretive he could be, that's the first time I heard he'd a house on this island.'

'Did he invite you to stay with him?'

'No, he very carefully didn't.' Prade finished his coffee, drew on the cigarette. 'I just didn't understand that! I mean, there he was, asking me to join him on the boat trip, yet there was no invitation to stay at his place. If he couldn't stand his secrecy being breached, how come I was asked on the boat?'

Alvarez stubbed out his cigarette. He'd been so certain that if he could identify Short's friend, the friend would be able to tell him sufficient about Short's background for him to be able to judge whether the death was, in fact, connected to the other two . . . Prade had been able to tell him nothing other than that Short had been strangely secretive. He said wearily, now not believing there was anything further to be learnt: 'What happened on Monday when he met you at the airport?'

'I was surprised to see him because the arrangement had been that he'd get in touch at the hotel. But he said he'd drive me to his place and we'd have drinks before he ran me out to the hotel, so I went back and found the courier and told her what was happening.'

'You drove straight to his house?'

'That's right. We had some drinks and he showed me round the place: I was quite tired but I had to look at absolutely everything. And I don't mind admitting that when I saw the empty bedrooms I wondered again why he couldn't have asked me to stay with him — it would have saved me a few quid . . . Still, that's history. In the end, he drove me all the way back here. Said he'd pick me up fairly early in the morning because he wanted a good start. I had the earliest breakfast I could bully the staff into giving me and then sat around.'

Alvarez thought for a moment, then said: 'Did Señor Short have any physical peculiarities, such as scars?'

'I never saw any. But then I never saw him stripped.'

'Were his teeth his own?'

'That's one hell of a question—after all, we didn't share a bedroom! . . . Though, come to think of it, I do seem to remember him once mentioning his teeth were soft and always giving trouble.'

'What about gold fillings?'

Prade was silent for a moment, then he said: 'I'm pretty certain one of his front teeth was gold-backed. You noticed it when he smiled.'

'Was this in his upper or lower jaw?'

'God knows! . . . And what's it matter?'

'I have to confirm that it was he who died in the boat.'

'Can't you tell by looking at him?'

'He was too severely burned for any normal visual identification.'

'Oh!' For the first time it seemed Prade realized how serious the fire had been.

'Do you know if he wore a ring?'

'Yes, he did. Some kind of signet ring that was too big for my taste.'

'Can you say what kind of design the signet had?'

'No. No way.'

'One last thing, señor. Would you be kind enough to let me take your fingerprints?'

'Would I what?'

'I will need them to help identify Señor Short, by elimination.'

'I don't like it, and that's straight. Fingerprints are . . . To us British, they're a bit of an emotive issue: police state and all that sort of thing. But I'll give them if it'll really help.'

'You are very kind. Please wait here while I return to my car for the necessary equipment.'

Ten minutes later, after thanking Prade for all his help, Alvarez left.

CHAPTER 13

At 6.36 that afternoon, Professor Fortunato's secretary rang from the Institute of Forensic Anatomy in Palma.

'Inspector Alvarez? The Professor has asked me to give you preliminary details of the post mortem on Señor Peter Short.

'The deceased was aged between twenty-five and forty years of age and was one metre eighty-two or eighty-three in height. It has proved impossible to determine the colour of his hair or eyes. He had at no time suffered any major fracture or undergone any major internal surgery.

'There are no signs of injuries other than those consistent with an explosion, but because of the extent of tissue destruction it is impossible to state categorically that he received no others.

'Analysis of his stomach contents shows that he consumed a meal four to six hours before his death and his blood alcohol ratio was just over point one per cent — in other words, he would have been influenced by the alcohol, but would not have been drunk.

'His teeth show signs of regular and frequent attention and the pattern of fillings has been taken. The second front tooth of the upper jaw had at some stage become badly chipped and a gold backing introduced: the quality of this dental work was high.

'Because his right hand must have been partially under his body much of the time, it did not suffer such severe tissue destruction as most of the rest of his body. It has thus proved possible to obtain subdermal prints of his third and fourth fingers. Copies are being sent to you.

'The Professor is of the opinion that the deceased met his death in an explosion and the subsequent fire.'

Alvarez was closing the shutters in his office when the phone rang. It was still rather early for him to be stopping work for the day so, reluctantly, he returned to the desk and answered the call.

'Superior Chief Salas has asked me to tell you,' said the woman with a plum in her mouth, 'that they have received a report from England. The passport number which you asked to be transmitted there is that of a passport which was stolen from the consular office in Mettram, northern Italy, just over a year ago. They are therefore unable to furnish any biographical details of the holder.'

'Then there's now no shadow of a doubt! Tell Señor Salas that the three deaths are connected, they're murder, and it's ten to one that somewhere along the line we're dealing with a criminal conspiracy.'

After replacing the receiver, he sat down behind the desk. By God, he thought, he'd been right all the time, even in the face of Salas's supercilious disbelief! So what now?

Clarke and Allen had known each other, but this fact had only come to light through the photograph Tracey had had. The third person in that photo had clearly not been Short, being a much older man. Was he, whoever he was, also connected with the conspiracy, whatever that was?

Short had had plenty of money. Assume he'd come into this as suddenly as had Clarke and Allen and then there were three men who'd become wealthy. The odds had to be that the source of this wealth was criminal. Yet Clarke and Allen did not have criminal records. How often did amateurs make a fortune from crime? In practical terms, and ignoring computer frauds, virtually never. Successful crime demanded hard experience and a mentality which had been brutalized into ignoring consequences. So here was a total contradiction.

Could anything fresh be learned from studying their backgrounds again? (This meant concentrating on Clarke and Allen — Prade had been able to tell him nothing about Short.) They came from very different backgrounds so was it odd that they'd known each other? Had they been on holiday when they first met? Had this holiday been the start of whatever it was that had led them to their fortunes? . . . But assuming that photo had been taken in Mallorca (Allen's wife had said her husband had been to the island for holidays), how could they, as foreigners, commit any but the simplest, and therefore unrewarding, crimes without being found out or betrayed?

Sweet Mary, a man's mind could only accept so many questions before it was in danger of exploding, like an over-revved engine. He leaned down and opened the bottom right-hand drawer of the desk.

She had the body of a woman five years younger and this without rigorous dieting. Rightly proud of it, she loved him to exclaim over it as he stroked her satiny flesh.

He ran his fingers down the small of her back, so lightly that he felt the brush of down.

'Do you know what you're doing to me?' she murmured. 'I'm purring. I'm a cat in front of the biggest saucer of cream in the world. I'm so happy that it's like a hundred sunbeams inside me.'

He leaned over until he could substitute his lips for his fingers. Then, suddenly, he stopped.

'What's the matter?' she asked.

He resumed. It was hardly the moment to admit that he'd suddenly realized that package holidays often catered for particular pleasures or hobbies . . .

CHAPTER 14

Alvarez stood in his office and stared down at the photograph on his desk. Clarke, Allen, and an unidentified older man, stood on a beach ringed by palms, beyond which were several many-storeyed, tourist-styled buildings which were backed by stark mountains, the peaks of two of which were unusually shaped.

A typical holiday snap, taken anywhere, any time within the past twenty years wherever tourists found sun and sea. But two things about this snap were of particular interest and might just possibly help to identify the location and the time: the two mountain peaks which leaned towards each other as if to touch and form a circle, and the oxygen bottles in a harness which rested on the sand in front of Allen. Surely there must be someone who'd be able to recognize that skyline? Scuba-diving was very popular in certain parts of the island and it was a sport which brought together people from widely different backgrounds.

He drummed on the desk with his fingers. Who did he know who'd been all over the island and had a good memory? His fingers stilled. Manuel Rotger.

The hotel Parelona was justly world famous. In an age of rapidly falling standards it tenaciously held to those of more spacious days: couples when booking in were expected to give the same surname, at dinner guests usually wore dinner-jackets or long dresses, bedlinen and towels were changed every day, and the staff were polite.

The doorman socially classified Alvarez with one quick glance, but even so he still opened the swing door with gloved hand and said gravely: 'Good morning, señor.'

Alvarez crossed the marble-floored lobby to the reception desk, behind which stood the receptionist, a tall, thin German, who spoke six languages fluently, dressed in black coat and striped trousers despite the heat, and Rotger, in the hotel uniform of deep pink coat and black trousers.

Rotger had been head concierge at the Parelona for fourteen years and in that time he had developed a generous waistline and a commanding presence. A great man, he had learned to deal with even the most tricky emergency with complete aplomb. Once, a well-known member of a royal family had, when by the pool, started howling and ripping off ladies' costumes. Rotger, hastily called to the scene, had walked him along and introduced him to a wealthy widow from Detroit who'd been making life hell for an unusually handsome waiter. The royal was not heard to howl again.

Alvarez asked Rotger if they could have a quick word together somewhere private and Rotger gracefully inclined his head, then led the way into a small office immediately beyond the reception area.

'How are things going?' asked Alvarez, as he sat.

'I can't complain,' replied Rotger. Many of the hotel guests would not have complained had they been as wealthy as he.

'And the family's well?'

'Very well, thank you.'

'What's the score — four kids?'

'Five. We had a girl at the beginning of the year.'

'Not retiring yet, then?'

Rotger smiled his I-am-not-very-amused smile. He now judged that this visit was not likely to embarrass him personally and therefore saw no reason to be amused by a boorish remark.

'I'd like you to do something for me.'

'I shall be only too pleased to help in any way I can,' he

answered automatically.

'Look at this, will you.' Alvarez brought the photograph out and passed it across. 'Was it taken on this island, and if so, whereabouts?'

Rotger briefly studied the photo. 'Don't you realize this could be anywhere in the Mediterranean where those package holidays go?' He spoke the words 'package holidays' in tones of contemptuous dislike.

'I know. It needs a miracle to identify the place. But I was told that if anyone in the world could work that miracle, you could.'

Rotger nodded.

'You must have been all over the island and you've a memory like an encyclopaedia.'

He put on a pair of spectacles and examined the photograph very much more carefully than before. 'The beach, the trees, the hotels . . . impossible to tell. But those mountain crests . . .' He took off his spectacles and replaced them in the case. He leaned back in the chair, joined his fingertips together, and then gripped his upper lip between his two forefingers and plucked it repeatedly, to the accompaniment of plopping noises. 'I seem to remember that unusual formation. I can recall looking at it and thinking that if the two crests had been just a bit larger they could have joined together to form a hole: a whole mountain.' He smiled, appreciating so sophisticated a witticism.

'Then it is on this island?'

'Indeed.'

'Where?'

He plopped his lip a few more times. 'Playa del Xima,' he said finally.

'Would that part of the coast be any good for scuba-diving?'

'It's where they held the championships a year or two back.'

Xima was a small village (nevertheless, more than four thousand people lived in it) which had been built around the top of an oblong hill to give protection from raiding Moors. One of the last battles between Moors and Christians on the island had been fought at the base of the hill and this anniversary was celebrated every June 10th. The Moors had inflicted heavy casualties and had only turned back because a storm had suddenly blown up and put their boats in danger, but because of the need for artistic balance they were now, every June 10th, routed and slaughtered.

Playa del Xima was three kilometres away. Once a low, unspoilt, beautiful stretch of coast, it was now a forest of concrete buildings.

Alvarez parked his car on the front by a bulbous palm tree, and climbed out. He looked to the east and there, many kilometres away but looking close in the clear air, were the two mountain crests which leaned towards each other. Now to identify the spot from which the photograph had been taken.

Some twenty-five minutes later he was talking to the assistant manager of one of the largest hotels on the front. The assistant manager, pot-bellied, harassed, unable to keep still for very long, said: 'Yes, that's us: taken before we had the extra floors put on which was a couple of years back.' He put the photograph down on his desk, then almost immediately picked it up again.

'I'm trying to identify the oldest man.'

'He's never been on the staff here, that's for certain.'

'He could have been a guest — the other two were — but I think it's more likely that he was an instructor. D'you see the scuba gear in front?'

The assistant manager brought the photograph slightly closer to his eyes. 'Yes, if you mean the two air tanks?'

'It's possible that he was the instructor and the other

two were on a package tour which specifically catered for anyone interested in scuba-diving.'

'As a matter of fact, the Hotel Bahia—that's the next but one to us—used to deal with a firm which specialized in clients who were interested in diving.'

'You said, used to deal with—have they stopped?'

'According to what I've heard. The hotel decided the custom wasn't large enough and the organizing firm wanted very cheap holidays.'

'But the Hotel Bahia will have the records?'

'What records?'

'The name of the instructor and of all the guests who've come out with the firm?'

The assistant manager smiled tiredly. 'It's most unlikely. If any of us had to keep those kinds of records for more than a year, we'd have to build somewhere to house 'em.'

'Damn! But it'll be worth asking, anyway . . . Look, could you do me a favour and ring them and ask?'

The assistant manager telephoned the other hotel, spoke to his opposite number, wrote briefly, then replaced the receiver. 'I'm afraid it's like I said. They don't keep detailed lists of guests for more than the year required by law and there's no way in which they can help you name someone from several years back. But they do have a record of the name of the travel firm which used to cater for diving enthusiasts and they've given it to me.' He passed a slip of paper across. 'And they suggest you get on to the Hotel Azul, at the other end of the beach. They're now dealing with that particular firm.'

The Hotel Azul was a small, one star hotel, set three roads back from the front. Potted rubber trees grew on either side of the reception desk and a segmented, very spiny cactus, its withered air roots making it look geriatric, was trained up the side of the archway over the main staircase on the far side of the lobby.

The receptionist, a young man, nodded. 'Yeah, that's right. We deal with a British firm which specializes in scuba-diving.'

'Is there an instructor?'

'Yep. Looks after all the gear and takes the people out diving and sees not too many of 'em drown! Not employed by us, of course.'

Alvarez brought the photograph from his pocket. 'Is this the instructor—the eldest of the three?'

'No. A much younger bloke.'

'How long's he been doing the job?'

'Ever since I've been working here and that's two years.'

'Is there someone who'd know who was the instructor before the present man?'

'The manager probably does. Hang on while I go and ask him.'

'Take the photo with you and see if he can identify the man.'

The assistant manager returned in less than two minutes. 'That's the first instructor, all right. The manager says they changed something like a year before I moved here.'

Three years ago: the same period that marked the time when Clarke and Allen had suddenly become wealthy. Alvarez knew the heady satisfaction of someone who had long pursued a distant objective and, against all the odds and despite endless disappointments, at least seemed to be in sight of his goal.

Garcia liked himself. There was no doubt on that score. Whenever he had a free moment, he walked up and down the beach in his very brief trunks displaying his bronzed, muscular body. Any attractive and unaccompanied woman became a target and such was his degree of self-satisfaction that if she turned down his advances he judged her a fool without taste.

Alvarez disliked him on sight, but initially managed to hide this fact. He introduced himself. 'Is it right that you take people out and teach 'em scuba-diving?'

'Sure.' Garcia smiled at two women who sat on rush mats on the sand and were looking in his direction.

'Did you ever meet the man who did the job before you?'

'What if I did, dad?'

'Then I want to hear about him.'

'Some other time maybe. I'm busy,' he said, as one of the women smiled back at him.

'You'd rather I took you in and held you as a material witness?'

'Hey — there's no call to be like that.' Garcia's contempt for this slack-bodied, middle-aged man gave way to the uneasy realization that although he'd be laughed out of a Mr World contest, he was after all a detective.

'Then perhaps you'll tell me when you met him?'

'When he quit. Bloody old fool. Tried to teach me the job just because he'd been diving since the Ark was salvaged.'

'How long ago was this?'

'Three years.'

Alvarez produced the photograph. 'Is he in this?'

'That's him.'

'What's his name?'

'I can't remember.'

'Try harder.'

A couple came and stood close to them and clearly wanted a word with Garcia. Alvarez nodded and Garcia went over and spoke to them, looked at his watch and at Alvarez, shook his head. The man asked a couple of questions, then he and his wife walked away. Garcia returned.

'Have you remembered his name?' Alvarez asked.

'He was a Frenchman. Always dressed like a tailor's dummy and thought himself a ladies' man. His name was something like Massif . . . Massier, that's it. Seemed to reckon he'd bloody well invented scuba-diving.'

'What happened to him after he quit here?'

'I wouldn't know.'

'Why did he quit?'

'I don't know that either. Look, all that happened was, I'd done a lot of diving, especially when I was doing my military service, and so when I heard the job was going I came along. And I was good, so I got it.'

'What time of the year was this?'

'August.'

'You're saying he left in the height of the season?'

Garcia sniggered. 'That's what got everyone really steamed up. Tourists coming out for the diving and no one to check the gear or hold their hands . . . The firm was screaming for someone. That's how I screwed 'em for a solid wage.'

'What happened when you took over?'

'He handed me the keys of the place where the equipment's kept, tried to tell me what to do, and then was away. Got a bit of skirt all lined up, like as not.'

'And that's the last time you saw him?'

'That's right.'

'You're quite certain?'

'Haven't I just said . . . No, as a matter of fact, that's not right. I've just remembered. I did see him once more, the next day. And was that a surprise!'

'Why?'

'Because he was sitting at a café with old Loco Llobera.'

'Why was that so strange?'

'Because the Frenchman was all smart and dainty and old Loco was a bag of rags who smelled like a midden.'

'Any idea whether Señor Massier is still on the island?'

'None at all.'

'D'you keep records of the names of people who come out and go diving?'

'Have to. The bloody firm makes me keep a log on what progress everyone makes and what standards they reach so that if they come out again I know all about 'em. PR exercise, they call it: a bloody waste of time, I call it.'

'How far do the records go back?'

'The year dot, judging by the dust.'

'I want to see them.'

CHAPTER 15

There were many restaurants along the front at Playa del Xima and without exception they catered for the tourists: three roads back was a small dingy-fronted restaurant which catered for the locals—and those few tourists who had the wit to eat there—where the food was excellent and it cost only half as much.

Alvarez regretfully put the last forkful of suckling pig in his mouth. It was a dish which varied enormously in quality, even at the same restaurant, and this had been one to dream about. He swallowed, looked down at his now empty plate, and sighed. He emptied the last of the wine from the earthenware carafe into his glass.

The waiter came and cleared his plate and asked him if he wanted a sweet. He chose banana with almonds. When these came, he peeled the banana and ate it and the toasted almonds alternately, but for once his mind was far removed from the food.

The records had been in a rusty filing cabinet in one corner of the lock-up garage that was used to store the diving gear and an air-compressor. Forty minutes after starting, he'd found what he wanted. July 5th to 18th:

Simon Allen, Peter Short, James Marsh, and Roger Clarke. Clarke and Allen had been in the photo, Short had not. But he was assuming that there was some connection between them so this surely meant that it was logical to include Marsh and, probably Massier . . .

Assume he'd identified the five men in the conspiracy, three of whom had been murdered. Murdered for what? Their share of the loot? What loot? No unsolved crime on the island three years ago had yielded the kind of money that was involved here. And in any case, hadn't he decided that, as amateurs, they couldn't have carried out a successful crime in the normal sense of the word . . . ?

The waiter returned to the table. 'D'you want anything more? A coñac?'

'Make it a large one.' Perhaps he could drown his sense of frustration. How many times now had he made some progress in the case, only to come up against the question: where had the money come from?

It was time to make an inspired guess, he thought as the waiter brought him a brandy. The four Englishmen had been from different backgrounds (at least, it seemed likely they had: nothing at all was yet known about Marsh), but one thing they'd obviously had in common had been a restricted budget — otherwise they'd have been on a more luxurious package. Massier had thrown up his job at the height of the season, when he'd have been making the money which would normally have kept him through the winter, so something suddenly and unexpectedly had happened to enrich him. The two events had to be connected. In other words, the source of Massier's good fortune and theirs was the same. Taking that one stage further, since Massier had been an expert diver and they had come out on a diving holiday, what more likely than that they had discovered their fortune through diving?

Drugs, as he'd originally considered? Consignments of

drugs were often dropped into the sea off the shore of the country into which they were to be smuggled, to be picked up later. Perhaps the five, when out diving, had found a considerable quantity of heroin or cocaine, had taken it ashore, and had subsequently sold it for large sums of money. Now, the men to whom it had been consigned but who had lost it, were extracting their revenge... But amateurs couldn't peddle drugs and hope to escape attention and there'd been no reports of unusual drug activity...

The waiter came near the table. Alvarez ordered another coñac.

He drank slowly, irritated because some memory, important in the present context, was knocking at his mind but refusing to enter. Something he'd heard very recently... Of course! Garcia had said that the last time he'd seen Massier, Massier had been drinking with a man called Loco Llobera, a stinking old bag of rags. Yet Massier had been a very fastidious man, over-conscious of his appearance, and normally not the kind of person to consort with a tramp...

He called the waiter across.

'Another coñac?' asked the waiter, with the tired disinterest of someone who'd spent much of his life serving food and drink to people who ate and drank too much.

'D'you know a man called Llobera: Loco Llobera?'

'No, I don't know him. On account of the fact that he died three years back.'

The guardia post had been built within the past couple of years so there were as yet few visible signs of structural decay and only one outer wall was cracked. Administrative quarters were to the front, living quarters to the rear. The office open to the public was to the left of the main entrance and here a guard sat and watched television, resenting any interruption.

'Inspector Alvarez, Cuerpo General de Policia, from Llueso.'

The guard scratched his right ear. Alvarez sat down on one of the chairs. 'I want a run-down on a man called Llobera who died three years ago.'

'I wasn't posted here then,' said the guard quickly.

'But I expect you can find someone who was?'

The guard muttered something, waited until the commercials began on the television, then came to his feet and left. When he returned, he said: 'The sergeant'll be along,' after which he slumped down in his chair and watched the television once more.

The sergeant was equally unfriendly, but there was nothing significant in this. Guards were never posted to the part of the country in which they'd been born and brought up, so none of them was an islander: like everyone from the Peninsula, they regarded the islanders as foreigners and disreputable ones at that.

'I'm interested in a man who died three year ago—used to be known as Loco Llobera,' said Alvarez.

'I remember him,' said the sergeant, slurring and swallowing his words in true Andalusian style.

'What can you tell me about his death?'

'What's there to tell? He was as pissed as a newt and fell over the cliffs at Setray.'

'The PM said he'd been tight?'

'PM? Who needed a PM? There was an empty bottle to show what had been going on before he fell over and broke his neck. And done himself proud, too: a bottle of French cognac.'

'Had anyone seen him there, drinking?'

'It sounds like you don't know the cliffs at Setray?'

'I don't.'

'They're a couple of kilometres from anywhere.'

'Then why was he there?'

'How should I know?'

'Didn't anyone ask that question?'

'If a drunk falls and kills himself, you don't spend days investigating his death. There's no call for that.'

'What time of the year was this?'

'End of August, beginning of September.'

'There was never any suggestion it mightn't have been an accident?'

'No.'

'How old was he?'

'The family said he was sixty-four. To look at him, he was a hundred and sixty-four. Filthy old sod! I had to help carry the body round and up and I didn't get the stink out of my nostrils for weeks.'

'Why was he known as Loco Llobera?'

'Why d'you think? He was crazy.'

'In what way?'

'How many ways are there? You're either crazy or you aren't . . . I did hear it was because he got a bullet in the head during the war.'

'Was he dangerous?'

The sergeant laughed contemptuously. 'Him! He was just soft: always giggling at nothing.'

'D'you know if he did any scuba-diving?'

'I know he hadn't been near water in thirty years.'

'What kind of family is left?'

The sergeant shrugged his shoulders.

'But there was one three years ago. Could you get me their address?'

The sergeant said belligerently: 'He died because he was so pissed he walked over the edge of the cliff. That's all. So why keep asking so many questions?'

'There's a chance he didn't fall, he was pushed.'

The sergeant walked past Alvarez, his expression angry. When a man's death had officially been held to be accidental only a fool Mallorquin would ever start asking questions about it.

THREE AND ONE MAKE FIVE

*

The finca lay two kilometres back from the beach. At the end of a short dirt-track, among small fields which were bounded by dry stone walls, was the house, squat, of the most elementary design, and in need of repair. Yet because it had been built with stones taken from the fields as these were cleared, with wood grown locally, and with roof tiles made of clay dug half a kilometre away, it was part of the countryside, something which a modern and superficially more attractive house could never be.

Alvarez parked alongside a pigsty in which several pigs were snorting and squealing. Come the winter, he thought as he climbed out of the car, and there would be a matanza with a pig slaughtered and the family and their friends preparing hams, sobrasada, butifarra, negro...

To the right of the house, a couple were working in the nearest field. He was dressed in beret, shirt, torn trousers and plimsolls, and was weeding with a small hand hoe. She was dressed in a wide brimmed straw hat, a faded and shapeless cotton frock, and shoes made from canvas and strips of worn tyre, and was irrigating, using a mattock to open and close channels running between bush tomatoes.

The man straightened up and stared at Alvarez, his leathery, lined, stubbled face showing no expression. The woman continued irrigating.

'Señor Amengual?'

'Well?'

'I'd like a word.'

'Who are you?'

'Enrique Alvarez, from Llueso.'

Amengual hawked and spat. 'I've a cousin out there.' He spoke as if Llueso were hundreds of kilometres away. 'Name of Juan Sanchez.'

'Does he run a butcher's shop?'

'That's him.'

'He sells some good meat . . . I've come to talk about your wife's brother who died three years back.'

Amengual's expression became sullen and he bent down and resumed work, chopping the heads off the weeds with a rhythm that he could maintain all day.

'Cuerpo General de Policia.'

The woman suddenly stopped work and stared at Alvarez and the water, rushing into the side channel from the main one which led back to an estanque, filled it and overflowed. Hastily she bent down once more and opened the entrance to the next channel, using the plug of earth to dam the previous one.

Amengual stopped his weeding and walked between the rows of sweet peppers to a rough pathway. When close to Alvarez, he jerked his head in the direction of the house.

Outside the house was a rough patio — a hard-packed dirt floor and concrete pillars, chipped and cracked, which supported wires on which were trained three grape vines whose dozens of bunches of grapes, now no larger than peas, hung down. Three wooden chairs and a table, all badly worm-eaten, were set out under the vines. Without a word, Amengual sat and stared out at the land.

'I'm sorry to have to bring up a sad subject,' said Alvarez, 'but I need to know certain facts about your wife's brother, Augustín Llobera, who died three years ago . . . Why had he gone out to the cliffs at Setray? What was he doing there, so far from anywhere?'

Amengual shrugged his shoulders.

'You must have some idea why he was there?'

Amengual spoke angrily. 'He fell and died. Does it matter why he was there to fall?'

'I need to know.'

A small cur dog, with curled tail came round the corner of the house and approached them. He shouted

and it hurriedly retreated.
'He lived here with you, didn't he?'
'When he was here.'
'Was he often away, then?'
'He was daft,' said Amengual with the detachment of a man who had always accepted life as it was and not yearned for what was not. 'Sometimes he were here, sometimes he weren't.'
'Would he be away a long time?'
'Maybe.'
'Have you any idea where he used to go when he was away?'
'No.'
'Maybe he stayed with a friend?'
'He didn't have no friends.'
'Had he been with you immediately before he died?'
'Hadn't seen him for more'n a couple of weeks.'
'How did he manage to live when he wasn't with you?'
'Some folks'd give him scraps to eat. When he got too hungry, he'd come back.'
'Did he ever talk about meeting foreigners?'
'Why'd he want to talk about foreigners?'
'During the war he got shot in the head — was that soon after it started?'
'What's it to you? He's dead. Let the poor bastard rest in peace, seeing as he never had any when he was alive.'
'Did he often talk about what happened to him during the war?'
Amengual stood and went into the house. When he returned it was with an earthenware pitcher and two mugs. He filled the mugs with wine and passed one across. It was a strange gesture of companionship coming, as it did, immediately after his angry outburst.
Alvarez drank. The wine was like it had been when he was young and it had all been locally made: harsh and leaving behind a taste of hot, dusty bitterness.

'Which army was he in?'

'He weren't in the army.'

'Then how'd he get shot?'

Amengual's expression tightened. He drained his mug, refilled it.

Over forty years ago, Alvarez thought, and still the fear and the guilt remained for some of those who had lived through the civil war, even though there was now a socialist government, the communist party was official, and La Pasionaria had appeared on television. 'Old man,' he said softly, 'no matter what happened then, it can't threaten you now.'

Amengual drank deeply, wiped his mouth with the back of his hand.

'Did he betray someone?'

'No,' he replied violently.

'Then how did he get shot?'

Amengual's wife, having finished irrigating the tomatoes, came across to the patio. She sat next to her husband.

'He's asking about Augustín,' Amengual said. 'About him being shot.'

She looked at Alvarez, but remained silent.

Alvarez waited, with the infinite patience of a peasant.

'Before it all started,' Amengual said suddenly, 'he was always talking.' He turned to his wife. 'Isn't that right? Before we was married, didn't I tell him, it's trouble to talk like that? But he wouldn't listen. Just kept on talking, didn't matter if they was listening.'

Alvarez pictured the times: the illiterate peasant denouncing the system under which the few lived lives of luxury and the many lived lives of poverty: the authorities who listened and waited: the men and women who were terrified by the words—knowing what reprisals they might bring—yet who were inexorably drawn to this vision of a future in which their lives might be granted some dignity . . .

'The guards came looking for him,' continued Amengual. 'He was twelve days in the mountains.'

'I took him food,' his wife said, speaking for the first time.

'Then he got clean away. The guards called the army, but they couldn't do no better. He got away!'

'They came to the house of my parents,' she said. 'They tried to make them talk, but they knew nothing so they could tell nothing. The guards left me because I was young, but it was me who knew where he was and was feeding him.'

They became silent, far away with their memories.

'He left the island?' Alvarez asked.

'He was a fisherman. So he took a boat and sailed to Barcelona and joined them.'

Them? There'd been so many factions to begin with: communists, anarchists, socialists . . . 'What did he do if he wasn't in the army?'

'The navy. Ain't I just said he was a fisherman?'

'The navy!' exclaimed Alvarez, seeing one more link with the five men who'd gone scuba-diving.

They were frightened by his sharp reactions.

He smiled as he held up his mug. 'Any chance of a drop more wine? Haven't had any so good since I was a kid and my parents made it.'

He talked about wine and wine-making and, because it had become obvious that first and foremost he was a peasant like themselves and not a detective, they gradually lost their fright.

'What ship was your brother on?' he asked.

'The *Aosta*,' she answered immediately. 'And he was on it when it came to Porto Cristo—not that any of us knew it . . .'

She talked about the invasion force, led by the old battleship *Jaime I*, which had sailed from Ibiza after the government had retaken that island. They'd arrived off Porto Cristo and the troops had landed and begun to fight their way inland . . .

'The Marqués de Orlocas lived in the big house. He was head of the local Falange.' Her voice was now very bitter. 'The girls couldn't get paid work except for going up to the big house: if they had looks, he was after them like a goat. And then if they got with child they were thrown out for sluts.'

'The brave Marqués de Orlocas!' sneered Amengual. He refilled both mugs, then passed his to his wife. When she'd drunk as much as she wanted, he topped it up for himself. 'So rich his lands stretched forever and his wife had more jewels than a field of wheat has ears. Ate their grub off gold. While the likes of us went hungry.' He drank, laughed harshly. 'When they told him the Red ships were off Porto Cristo and the soldiers were landing, his bowels turned to water. Some guards were sent to defend him, but he thought about the mothers of the women he'd raped and he reckoned an army wouldn't be big enough to defend him . . . He'd a boat what he kept at Puerto Britax. Never used it much on account of always being seasick, but it was smart to have a boat. He reckoned that it'd take him, his wife, and two bitches of daughters, to somewhere safe. So the guards drove him to the Puerto with all his valuables.

'When they reached the boat, he wouldn't take the guards with him because he reckoned there wasn't room with all his valuables. They said they'd be butchered if they was caught by the other side, but it was all the same to him what happened to them now. He sailed out of the bay and turned to Palma. Usually he had a bloke to do the engines and so he didn't know much about 'em . . .'

'And they broke down,' interrupted his wife eagerly and with deep gratitude. 'And they drifted and the wind and tide took 'em down the coast towards Porto Cristo.'

Amengual nodded. 'The *Aosta* was anchored offshore and beyond the other ships and because there was a moon someone saw the boat drifting by. It looked abandoned and the captain said as they ought to get hold of it to use for taking supplies ashore. Being a fisherman and knowing about small boats, Augustín was sent off in charge of one of the launches, along with three other seamen.

'They didn't see anyone was aboard until they was alongside. Then the Marqués showed himself and started pleading and promising 'em a fortune if they'd let him go. Never recognized Augustín. But Augustín recognized him, all right.

'The Marqués hadn't no balls, but his wife and daughters was different. They'd a couple of guns and as soon as they were certain Augustín and them others were from the Red ships, they started shooting. Two of the seamen was killed and Augustín was hit in the head. He was still conscious, so he sailed the launch out of gunshot, turned it, and then put it at full speed and aimed it slap at the Marqués's boat. They went into it so hard they smashed it and turned it over. Pretty soon it sank, taking the Marqués and two of the women with it. But one of the daughters scrambled aboard the launch, which was still floating even though it had been real smashed up . . . Augustín got 'em back to the ship before he lost consciousness.'

There was a silence. 'And then?' asked Alvarez.

'The next day the Italian planes started bombing and the other side counter-attacked and the soldiers got pushed back. The ships did what they could, but a lot of soldiers was killed or taken prisoner. And there wasn't much difference for the poor sods.'

'What happened to Augustín?'

'When his ship docked in Barcelona they put him in hospital. They did what they could for him, but he'd gone soft on account of the shot to the head.'

'And what about the Marques's daughter who'd survived the sinking of the boat?'

Amengual hawked and spat. 'She lived. And later her side won so she was back and she started living in the big house again.'

'But not for long. With God's help, it caught fire,' said his wife, with simple but deep satisfaction.

Amengual spoke with renewed bitterness. 'But no one, not even God, could burn up the fields. So they're still here . . .' He stopped and looked at Alvarez, frightened that the consequences of an arson committed by a village all those years before could still harm him.'

'The fields should have been salted,' said Alvarez harshly.

Amengual lifted the mug and drained it. He knew now, for certain and beyond question, that this man was a good peasant.

'Did the daughter try to recover the jewellery and gold which had been in the boat?' Alvarez asked.

'She tried.' Amengual refilled his mug. 'She spoke to all her powerful friends and they found out who'd been the fourth seaman in the launch. He was asked, where was the boat when the destroyer's launch rammed it?' He sniggered. 'He'd been drafted in from Madrid, on his first voyage, not knowing one end of a ship from t'other: hadn't an idea where the boat went down. So then she hired divers and they dived and dived and they found nothing.' He banged the table with clenched fist. 'Bloody nothing,' he exulted.

'When did Augustín return here?'

Amengual looked at his wife. He drank.

She spoke in little more than a whisper. 'It were four year before he came back and we were married by then. We'd asked, but he'd fought for them so no one cared and we thought him dead . . . But one day, when we was in that field over there . . .' She pointed. 'He came to speak to us and I never recognized him. Sweet Mary, I never recognized him!'

'But he recognized us,' said her husband.

'Was he very mentally upset?' Alvarez asked.

'He was daft,' replied Amengual directly, but compassionately.

'Did he remember much of what had happened to him during the war?'

Neither of them answered.

'What did he say when you asked him about the time he was injured?'

'He just laughed,' she answered, with shame.

'Laughed?' repeated Alvarez, initially surprised.

She lowered her head.

Amengual said: 'The youngsters—them that was too young to have been in the fighting—used to say to him, "What was it like, invading your own land?" And he just laughed. And it became a game with 'em. Ask Loco what it was like to be shot in the head and see the silly bugger just laugh . . .'

'Did the Marqués's daughter get in touch with him when she heard he was back to learn if he knew where her father's boat had sunk?'

'Aye, she did that. Not herself, of course. But men came and asked him and even offered him money. And he just laughed at 'em.'

'Why did he laugh?'

They both stared at him. They'd explained everything. So how, unless he were mocking them, could he now ask so stupid a question?

'Did he ever explain to you why he laughed?'

'It was because he was a daftie,' replied Amengual defensively.

'But was he quite as stupid as he behaved? D'you think some of it could have been a camouflage?'

This completely bewildered them. The story of Augustín Llobera had become history. Now, the detective was asking them to go outside the boundaries of that history — this they could not do.

Alvarez stared beyond the patio at a patch of aubergines, the purple fruit forming a sharp contrast with the leaves. She had said: 'I never recognized him. Sweet Mary, I never recognized him!' And her husband had said: 'But he recognized us.' It was impossible now to judge how confused his mind had been, but at least one corner of it had obviously been relatively lucid . . . When people had asked him about the invasion, he'd just laughed and they'd taken this to be further proof of his loonyness. Who but a fool would laugh about such things? . . . Might not a fool who had discovered a way of gaining sweet revenge?

Ever since Llobera had started work — and in those days a boy had started very young — he'd been a fisherman. So he would have known the local waters like the back of his hand. During the invasion, when on a moonlit night he'd been sent off from the *Aosta* in the destroyer's launch to take the drifting boat in tow and had suddenly been fired at, he'd have known almost to the metre where he was. He'd been shot and the injury to his head had cost him much of his reason — but why shouldn't memories of the shooting, even in a confused state, have stayed with him?

He'd returned home four years later after God knows what privations and for the first time had learned that the Marqués de Orlocas had had the family fortune aboard that boat. He'd also have learned that the surviving daughter had done all she could to recover the jewellery and plate, but all attempts had failed because the sunken boat could not be found. And he'd have known where that boat lay. He could have told the Orlocas daughter and made himself some money — more money than he could ever hope to earn — but nothing on God's earth would make him help her, the last representative of a family he hated and who had injured him for life. No! He was going to hug his knowledge to himself and then one day he'd salvage the fortune and gloat over it and laugh and laugh because it was hers by legal right, but he had possession of it . . .

Then, probably when drink had upset his judgement even more than usual, he'd let slip a hint of the truth to a foreigner who was a scuba-diver . . .

CHAPTER 16

Alvarez did not get back to Puerto Llueso until nine that night. He parked opposite Tracey's flat, crossed the road, and climbed the stairs to her patio. She was not in and there was no note for him on the front door. She'd obviously decided to go and have a coffee at a café to while away the time until he arrived. He sat down on one of the patio chairs and stared out at the bay, looking as if washed by an impressionist's brush.

Night set in, at first almost imperceptibly, then seemingly suddenly. The lighthouse at the end of the eastern arm of the harbour began to flash and the street lighting was switched on. He checked the time. And suddenly he was hit by the icy fear that something had happened to her.

He returned to the road and walked along the front, checking the people who were sitting at the outside café tables, but did not see her. Then he looked in at several of the cafés which lay back from the front, but again he failed to find her. His alarm grew, but he tried to still it by telling himself that while he'd been away from the flat, she'd probably returned and was wondering what on earth had happened to him. He hurried back to the flat.

She still was not there. Going down the stairs once more, he tried to work out calmly and logically where to look for her assuming, as he must do now, she had met trouble . . .

'She's gone out,' said a woman in Mallorquin from inside the opened doorway of the lower flat. 'Left just after eight.' She stepped out: elderly, wearing a print dress and a delicate lace shawl over her shoulders, she had some knitting in her hand. 'She went off in a car.'

'Did she hire it?'

She said, with wicked pleasure: 'Do hire cares now come with a handsome driver?'

He longed to find out who the driver had been, but was not going to give her the satisfaction of asking. 'I expected them to be back by now,' he said, as casually as he could.

'Shall I tell her you were looking for her?'

'If you like.'

He said good-night and returned to his car. Who could Tracey have gone out with? And why hadn't she waited for him? He'd been late, but it hadn't been his fault and he had warned her . . .

When he arrived home, the family was watching a television quiz. He sat down with them and stared at the screen, but saw nothing of the show. Had Tracey ever mentioned knowing someone in the port? But hadn't she told him she'd come there simply to be with him? Then who . . .

'Hey, Enrique! Are you deaf, or something?' asked Dolores sharply.

He jerked his mind back to the present to find that the show had finished and the family were all staring at him.

'Or something,' chuckled Jaime.

'Be quiet!' She said to Alvarez: 'I said, have you had supper?'

'No, I haven't. But it doesn't matter.'

'Not hungry?' said Jaime. 'You know your trouble? You've been having too much . . .'

'Shut up!' snapped Dolores. Jaime looked at her resentfully, but did not complain aloud. Spain was still very much a country where the women were expected to treat the men with reverence, but when married to a woman of Dolores's nature there were times when it was expedient not to stress that fact.

'You'd better come through to the kitchen and I'll find you something,' she said.

'Please don't bother. I'm really not . . .' began Alvarez.

'I'm not having you go hungry in my house.' She left, to go through to the kitchen.

'Uncle, what is it you're having too much of?' asked Juan.

Jaime laughed as Alvarez followed Dolores.

In the kitchen, Dolores opened the refrigerator and brought out an earthenware bowl. 'I'll heat this up for you.'

'I really don't want very much.'

'You'll eat a square meal.' She put the bowl down on the cooker. 'Where d'you have lunch?'

'A restaurant in Playa del Xima.'

'Why'd you go there?'

'Because of the case.'

'You were on a case?'

'Why should I drive all that way if it wasn't work?'

'I just thought . . .' She stopped. She lit the gas under the bowl, then looked at him with a very concerned expression. 'Enrique, don't let yourself be hurt.'

'What d'you mean?' he demanded roughly.

She stirred the savoury rice. Men could be such fools it hurt to watch them.

On Saturday morning, Alvarez received a letter from the Palma Institute of Forensic Anatomy. Due to the fact that Short's right hand had not been burned as severely as most other parts of his body, it had proved possible to cut away the skin of the fingertips of the second and third fingers, treat these areas of skin with a formaldehyde solution, and then photograph, with an oblique light, the papillary pattern on the inner surface. Photographs were enclosed.

He searched the office for the case which contained the fingerprint equipment and eventually found it. He drove out to Ca Na Rostra, let himself into the house, and went through to the sitting-room. He put the case down on one of the occasional tables and brought out of it a bottle of fine black powder and a camel's-hair brush. He picked up each of the glasses on the silver tray in turn, by inserting two fingers inside and then splaying them as he upended the glass, and painted the powder over the outside surfaces. A large number of prints were raised, some of them clear, others too blurred or overlaid to be of any use. He checked the clear ones first against the record he had of Charles Prade's prints—those on one glass matched. Then he checked those on the second glass against the photographs and these matched.

Upstairs, in the only bedroom in which the bed was made up, he treated possible surfaces for prints and raised two sets, on a cupboard handle and on the dust-jacket of a book on the bedside table. They were different from Prade's, but matched both those on the second glass and those of the dead man.

Alvarez began to repack the equipment. Even his ever suspicious superior chief could not harbour any doubts now. The dead man was Short.

Alvarez returned to the guardia post. The building seemed hotter and stuffier than ever and by the time he'd climbed the stairs and reached his office he was sweating heavily and short of breath. He sat. Tomorrow, he promised himself, he'd start getting back into condition: no smoking, no drinking, and early morning jogging.

As soon as he was feeling better, he telephoned Salas's office. To his dismay, the plum-voiced woman said that Superior Chief Salas would speak to him.

'Well?' demanded Salas, 'what's gone wrong now?'

'Nothing's gone wrong, señor.'

'That makes for a welcome change.'

'You will remember I told you about the photograph of the three men, two of whom were Allen and Clarke, on an unknown beach? I managed to find a way of tracing the location of that photograph. I remembered that the head concierge of the Hotel Parelona is a man who's travelled all over the island . . .'

'Would you get to the point?'

Sadly, Alvarez realized that Salas was not interested in his series of brilliant deductions, only in the results. He gave them.

'It's taken you long enough to find all this out,' said Salas. 'But at least it must now be clear even to you that this man, Llobera, let slip the fact that he knew exactly where the boat had sunk and the five men, led by Massier, decided to search for it. They found it and the treasure and instead of declaring that to the authorities, stole it . . .'

'As I said at the beginning, señor . . .'

'Kindly don't interrupt. Llobera may have died in an accident or he may have been murdered: since it happened three years ago, we probably will never know for certain. However, we can be certain of what is happening now. One of the five men has determined to appropriate for himself the shares of all the others. Clarke, Short, and Allen, have all been murdered, in a manner which attempted to make it seem their deaths had been accidents.'

'I did suggest . . .'

'Will you let me finish? Since Marsh and Massier are still alive, in so far as we know, one of those two has to be the murderer. I must confess that, in spite of experience, I am still surprised I have to explain all this to you.'

'But, señor, it was you who kept saying . . .'

'I suppose I'd better now detail what has to be done. The whereabouts of Marsh and Massier must be ascertained and they must be closely investigated to discover which of them is the murderer. At the same time, as much of the jewellery and plate as remains must be recovered and returned to the surviving daughter of the Marqués de Orlocas. Is that clear?'

'As a matter of fact, I have already . . .'

'Even you, inspector, should be unable to confuse and confound the issues now.'

Alvarez parked his car and crossed the road. As he approached the stairs leading up to Tracey's flat, he looked at the bead curtain which covered the downstairs doorway. He thought he caught a sign of movement. The old woman who lived there was watching and probably laughing to herself at the sight of him chasing after a foreigner.

He reached the patio to find Tracey stretched out face downwards on a Li-lo, sunbathing: the top half of her bikini was by her side. He knelt and kissed the back of her neck.

'That's nice. Do it again.'

As he kissed her a second time, he ran the tips of his fingers down her spine.

'That's even nicer. I'm purring loud and clear,' She turned over.

The patio was on a level with the windows of the house on either side and he hurriedly looked to see if anyone were watching.

'What's the panic?'

'Well . . .' He gestured at her bare breasts.

'For Heaven's sake! Surely you know that the beaches

are filled with bare tits?'

'You are not on the beach. And even if you were, I wouldn't like you to be undressed like this.'

'You wouldn't? And who the hell are you to start telling me what to wear?' She reached out and slid her hand up his right leg. 'Look, love, I've a thick head and I need humouring, not lecturing. So come and sit down and be extra nice to me.'

He sat on the edge of the Li-lo. He reached out and picked up the bikini top and handed it to her.

'You don't like my tits?'

'They're very beautiful, but . . .'

'But you can't bear to think of anyone else goggling at them? Typical male hypocrisy. See a bit of flesh on someone else and it's wonderful, see it on the woman you're with and it's panic stations.' She finally fitted on the bikini top and clipped it behind her back. 'Is that better?'

'Very much better.'

'I'll remember that the next time you want to play with them . . . I'm thirsty, so what say we have a drink?'

He stood. 'What would you like?'

'A sweet Martini with soda, masses of ice, and a large slice of lemon.'

The kitchen was in a muddle and it looked as if she hadn't washed up for several meals. He poured out two drinks, added ice to both, a sliver of lemon to hers, and carried them outside.

She sat up on the Li-lo and settled on one of the chairs. He cleared his throat. 'I came here last night, but you weren't in.'

'I waited, but in the end reckoned you must have forgotten.'

He spoke indignantly. 'How could you imagine I'd ever forget? I was over the other side of the island and couldn't get back here until nine.'

'I'll believe you.'
'Where were you?'
'Out.'
'But out where?'
'What's it matter?'
'I need to know.'
'For God's sake, forget it. Concentrate on telling me how much you love me and charm my headache away.'

He accepted that he ought to avoid an argument, but he could not contain his jealousy. 'The woman from the flat below said . . .' He stopped.

'What did the inquisitive old bitch say?'
'That you went off in a car with a man.'
'Well?'
'Did you go out with someone?'
'What if I did?'
'Who was he?'
'None of your business.'
'Indeed it is.'
'You listen to me. I'm over eighteen and single so I'll go out with whom I like, when I like.'
'You'd no right to go out with anyone else.'
'For God's sake! . . . Let's get one thing straight. You're not putting me in purdah, like you would one of your own women.'

'But we're . . .' He struggled to find the words he wanted and failed because he could not bring himself to admit that they were no more than lovers without any declared commitment to the future. Sick with jealous despair, he blundered on. 'Who was he? Someone you knew from Bahia Mocamba?'

'I never set eyes on him before last night.'
'You what?' he said, horrified.
'Now what's the trouble? Look, you never turned up. And I was feeling down, so I said to hell with it and went out for a drink. And while I was at the café a man started

talking and he was fun. So when he said, let's eat and try a disco afterwards, I said, why not? What's so dreadful about that?'

He was shocked that she could not realize how outrageous her behaviour had been.

Her tone hardened. 'So now you're wondering if I slept with him? If it makes you any better company, when we got back here he tried to come up but I told him, nothing doing. So he left.'

'But you went out with him even though you'd never met him before,' he said despairingly.

'You know something?' she said in a lower, softened voice. 'It's like trying to talk to someone who speaks a different language and no interpreter. I'm living in the present, you're living in the past. You reckon a man can have fun, but a woman's got to stay at home and die of boredom.'

'I thought you loved me.'

'Why d'you think I refused to let him come up?'

'But now you're saying . . . But for me and even though you'd only just met him . . .'

'Forget it, my very old-fashioned darling. Live for now, not yesterday, not tomorrow. Grab what's going and to hell with anything else.'

He shook his head.

'Come on, it's easy when you've learned how.' She leaned over and kissed him. After a while, he cared only about now.

CHAPTER 17

Sticky from the heat, Alvarez slumped back in the chair in his office. Despite Salas's curt, ungracious summation of the case, there were two, not one, possible motives for the murders: self-preservation or gain. Self-preservation? Perhaps either Marsh or Massier had had reason to fear that he was about to be betrayed. Yet if that were so, then either he'd no clear idea of who the potential betrayer was or he believed that Clarke, Short and Allen, were in the conspiracy to betray him. Either possibility seemed unlikely. And would someone betray him when to do so must be to expose to the authorities (if the deaths were not accepted as accidental) the fact that the Marqués de Orlocas's fortune had been recovered? (Hadn't Llobera almost certainly been murdered in order to prevent his stupidly giving away the slightest hint of what had happened?) Gain? There were five of them to share the fortune. From all accounts, the jewellery and plate had been of such quality and in such quantity that to have sold it all at once would have been to draw attention to it, whereas a piece or two could be sold from time to time without undue comment. Then the odds must be that the bulk of it was still hidden somewhere. Five of them each owned a fifth of this. Allen's wife had had no knowledge of it and this suggested, as was logical, that each man had been sworn to total secrecy. In these circumstances, the death of one man must mean his share would go unclaimed or, to put it another way, on the death of one man what was left would be divided amongst the survivors. So the murderer stood to gain the whole fortune for himself . . .

Where would the jewels and plate be hidden? They'd want to be within easy reach of their fortune. Clarke and Allen had lived on the island, Short had owned a house here and had been a frequent visitor. But in an age when air travel was so quick and simple, to be near to something did not necessarily mean one had to be physically near to it. So it was perfectly feasible to imagine that neither Marsh nor Massier was living on the island. Where would they be if they weren't? The Peninsula? France? Germany?

He picked up a pencil and began to make notes. Requests would have to be made to all possible countries for information on the present whereabouts of James Marsh and Raymond Massier. A photograph of Massier could be provided, but they'd no description of Marsh. Still, if Marsh were not living in the UK, but in a country where everyone had to have some form of identity card, it should be reasonably simple to trace him.

He put the pencil down, sighed, rubbed his forehead. This was going to involve a great deal of work. But with any luck, not too much of it should fall on his shoulders.

Palma phoned on Friday morning. Salas's secretary said: 'The superior chief has asked me to give you the following message. The police in Nice have informed us that a James Marsh, an Englishman, is living in Pelonette. Do you know where that is?'

'No, señorita.'

'It is a village nine kilometres inland from Nice,' she said, in a tone of voice which suggested that every educated person knew exactly where Pelonette was.

'Then we must ask the French police to . . .'

'It will be necessary for Señor Marsh to be questioned.'

'Yes, of course. So if we . . .'

'You are to fly to Nice.'

'I'm what?'

'The flight has been booked.'

'It's . . . it's impossible.'

'Are you ill?'

Perhaps, he thought, he was ill. What else could explain why his mind should suddenly fill with the blurred picture of a man, much younger than he, returning with Tracey to her flat and this time not being refused . . .

'Well, Inspector?'

'Señorita, I am far too busy to be able to leave here.

Surely we can ask the French police to carry out the preliminary interrogation . . .'

'If you wish to query the order,' she said with schoolmistress primness, 'you must do so with Superior Chief Salas, not with me.'

Salas's voice was loud and clear. 'Absolute nonsense.'

'Señor,' protested Alvarez, 'I really am overwhelmed with work. I've countless serious crimes under investigation.'

'Really? I don't remember receiving your preliminary reports?'

'I've been too busy to make them,' Alvarez said weakly. 'Señor, if I go to France and am not here to continue with all these investigations, what will happen?'

'They might stand a chance of being solved . . . You are booked on a plane tomorrow morning. Is that quite clear?'

As they came in to land, Alvarez closed his eyes. There was a thump from underneath him as some large and vital piece of the plane fell off; the engines' notes changed as they prepared to flame out; as he braced himself for the crash he cursed the woman next to him who was so fat that it would be difficult to clamber over her in his desperate rush to the emergency exit . . . They landed and the engines went into reverse thrust and they slowed. He opened his eyes and gazed with astonishment at the world.

The Customs and immigration checks were perfunctory and within twenty minutes of landing he walked out of the baggage area.

'Monsieur Alvarez?'

He turned. 'That's me,' he said in French.

'Wonderful—you speak French! My Spanish is like my German—I don't have any. Welcome to France. Now let me introduce myself. Officier Pierre Danois, of the regional Police Judiciare, Sûreté Nationale. In other words, a dogsbody.' He was in his mid-twenties, well built but not tall, with a long face whose expression was normally one of light-hearted and irreverent amusement.

'Here, let me have your case.'

'Don't bother, thanks. It's only an overnight bag with some washing tackle in case I can't return today.'

'Then let's get moving. I've a car outside and we can drive straight out to Pelonette.'

They walked across to the nearest glass swing doors, passing a franchised counter which sold perfumes and specialized toilet articles, and out to the pavement. A green Renault 14 was parked immediately by a No Parking sign. Once they were seated in this, Danois produced a pack of cigarettes. 'Do you use these, Monsieur Alvarez?'

'I do, thanks. And please, the name is Enrique.'

Danois helped himself to a cigarette and used the car lighter to give them both a light. He pulled open the ashtray but then, instead of driving off, settled back in the seat. 'Something's happened which I'm afraid is going to complicate matters for you. Marsh died last night.'

'Sweet Mary!' Alvarez exclaimed in Spanish.

'It looks like an accident.'

'But it wasn't.'

'You seem very sure?'

'I am.' So now there was only the Frenchman, Raymond Massier, left and by being the sole survivor he had identified himself as the murderer. And Alvarez suddenly remembered the one-franc coin found in Clarke's car and the empty bottle of French cognac at the point on the cliffs from which Llobera had fallen and he knew with a sense of shame that he ought to have named the murderer before now . . . A murderer who would not yet know that the murders had been identified as such, but would believe they'd all been accepted as accidents, so that he would be off his guard . . .

'He fell out of an upstairs window and landed on his head on a flagstone. His ex-boyfriend' Danois's tone became contemptuous 'found him this morning at around nine o'clock and by then he'd been dead for some hours. Before his death he'd obviously been drinking. The preliminary investigation was completed just before I came here to fetch you and I think it's safe to say that but for you his death would have been put down as an accident. But you say it definitely wasn't?'

'I can tell you one more thing that's certain. Before he died, he had a visitor, a Frenchman by the name of Raymond Massier. Massier deliberately got him drunk and then pushed him out of the upstairs window.'

Danois started the engine and pulled away from the kerb. 'Can you fill in a bit of the background for me?'

Alvarez gave him a brief résumé of all that had happened as they drove away from the airport and headed inland.

Danois stubbed out his cigarette. 'Then as I see things, we've two facts to establish. First, that the dead man is the same James Marsh who was in the holiday group that went diving in Mallorca and found the treasure. Second, that his death wasn't an accident.'

'He was murdered. Each death has been made to look like an accident, but it has been murder.'

'I'm not arguing, but have you been able to prove beyond all shadow of a doubt that any of the three deaths—or four, if you count the poor devil who was shot up in the war and fell over the cliff—was murder?'

Alvarez hesitated, then spoke reluctantly. 'Not if one takes each death separately. But look at them all together . . .'

'We French can be very provincial, Enrique. We've only this one death on French soil. We'll consider your cases in relation to this one, of course, but . . . Well, obviously one of the things that'll help will be the proof that this death is directly connected with the others. D'you have a photograph of Marsh together with any of the other men who've died?'

'No.'

'Is there anyone who can swear he knew any of them?'

'After three years . . .' Alvarez shrugged his shoulders.

'Oh well! Perhaps we'll turn up something that'll help. So far, the house hasn't been thoroughly searched so we'll take care of that.'

'Has the body been removed?'

'It has, but naturally only after photographs had been taken and the police doctor had examined it.'

'Did he have anything to say?'

'Only that the injuries were fully consistent with having fallen from the upstairs room.'

They came up behind a heavy-load lorry and with Gallic exuberance Danois pulled out on a near-blind bend. Alvarez, who as a driver would take the most appalling risks, closed his eyes and prayed with brief intensity. Nothing was coming in the opposite direction and they safely passed and continued at speed along the undulating road that bordered fields in which grew vines, citrus and apricot trees.

'You say you were certain—I mean, you would have been certain, but for me—that this was an accident. Did you not consider suicide?'

'There was no suicide note and no history of suicide threats. Admittedly there were emotional problems, but we reckoned these could have caused him to get tight and, when tight, not knowing what he was doing, he fell.'

'What kind of emotional problems?'

'I told you his boyfriend found him.' Danois's voice again became scornful. 'They'd been together for some time, but a few days ago they had a row and Guichard left.'

'Have you questioned Guichard?'

'Only in connection with the finding of the body. Although we did learn a bit about what went on beforehand. Guichard became friendly with another man and Marsh got to hear about it and started throwing jealous tantrums . . . If you think our lives can be complicated, you want to tune into theirs!'

'Was Guichard shocked by the death?'

'He certainly seemed to be.'

They passed through the village of Pelonette. A couple of dozen houses lined the road on either side and because the few windows facing the road were, without exception, shuttered, they gave the village an air of desolation. Beyond the village they passed a large vineyard, breasted a hill, continued halfway down on the other side and then turned into a narrow lane.

The house stood a hundred metres back from the lane. The roof tiles were the same 'Roman' tiles, it was stone built, and there were even limestone blocks capping the windows, yet it could never have been mistaken for a Mallorquin house. It was largely a question of proportions. On the island, the only guiding principles to any old building had been utility: here, where life had been kinder, there had been time to consider proportion and beauty.

They parked in front of the garage, a new, wooden building fifty metres from the side of the house, over which grew a luxuriant bignonia. A flagstone path led past flowerbeds to the front door.

'There's a well at the back and so there's plenty of water,' said Danois, as he looked briefly at the lawn. 'The gardener's been coming three times a week and, according to Guichard, Marsh spent most of his spare time working out here.'

It was an attractive garden. The undulations of the land had been used to great effect and there was the orderliness of formality, yet also the delight of the unexpected.

They went round the house, to a flagstone patio in one corner of which was a barbecue pit. 'That's where he fell from,' said Danois.

Alvarez looked up. The wooden-framed window was open, with the shutters clipped back. From it, there was a drop of just over four metres. Two of the flagstones underneath it were stained.

'We'll go upstairs in a minute and you'll see that the sill is only knee-high. If one's three parts tight and near the window, it wouldn't take much to fall out.'

'Or to be pushed out?'

'Equally true.'

'Was there any suggestion of the body having been moved at all?'

'No.'

'What was Marsh wearing?'

'T-shirt, cotton trousers, pants, and sandals.'

'Were there any bruises on his body, as opposed to the injuries to his head?'

'The police doctor didn't make a detailed examination, of course, but he didn't note any . . . There'll be a PM now. The pathologist is a difficult old sod, but I'll ask him to keep in mind bruises from being pushed over the sill . . . Shall we go in now?' Danois brought a key from his pocket. 'This is for the front door so we'll have to go back round.'

They entered a large room that was neither exclusively hall nor sitting-room, but whose character partook of both. Alvarez looked round at the small framed paintings, the delicately shaped, satin-covered chairs, the Dresden figures, the fussily elaborate tables, the pink curtains, and the pink and green carpet.

'Very elegant,' said Danois, making it clear what he thought of such elegance.

They went upstairs to the largest of the three bedrooms.

Here colours had been used in a manner that initially startled, then provoked either contempt or surprised admiration. The hangings of the tester were pink, yet the bedcover was a strong mauve: the bedcover had been turned down to reveal brick red sheets and puce pyjamas: there were two carpets, one lime green, the other a bright ochre: the wallpaper was red on two walls and blue on the others. There were four framed photographs, taken from different angles, of Michelangelo's David.

'No need to ask whether he was left or right-handed!' said Danois.

Alvarez went over to the single window, which opened inwards. It was easy to imagine a man, drunk, going to the window to try to clear his rocking head, leaning forward or swaying and losing his balance, and pitching over the low sill before he could gather his wits sufficiently to try and catch hold of something to save himself. By the same token, it was easy to visualize a second person coming up from behind and pushing . . .

'The only papers are down in the study,' said Danois. 'I expect you'd like to go through them?'

'Yes, I would. Not that I think you could have overlooked anything . . .'

'We could have overlooked everything since, as I said, we haven't yet looked very hard,' said Danois cheerfully.

The study was more simply, and for Alvarez much more pleasantly, furnished. Two walls were lined with shelves and these were filled with books, both hardback and paperback, there was a large desk, a couple of attractive rush-bottomed chairs, a bracket clock, a small piecrust table, with a beautiful patina, and two paintings in watercolours of local scenes.

'I've checked for a wall safe,' said Danois, 'but there isn't one.'

Alvarez went over to the desk and pulled open the drawers. Out of the eight, five were filled with files, cash books, and notebooks. 'There's a job here!'

Danois looked at his watch. 'It's coming up to apéritif time and in the next village there's a restaurant which ought to have three stars in Michelin but, thank God, hasn't so one can still afford to eat there. How about a meal and leaving all this until afterwards?'

It was not a question which needed to be asked twice.

It was just after six o'clock that evening when Alvarez opened a small notebook which, from the mass of brief, scrawled entries, the sets of figures written at all angles, and the fact it had been in the top left-hand drawer of the desk and the telephone was on the left-hand side of the desk, appeared to have been used as an aide-mémoire for the telephone. He slowly leafed through the pages, often having difficulty in deciphering the thin, scrawly writing. On one of the middle pages there was an entry, ringed with a thick pencil line, which read RM 0782. He said: 'I think I've found something.'

Danois, who'd been reading one of the few French paperbacks on the shelves, stood and crossed to the desk. He stared at the entry, picked out by Alvarez's stubby forefinger.

'RM is Raymond Massier,' said Alvarez.

'And the figures?'

'A telephone number which with any luck will lead us straight to Massier.'

'What exchange?'

'Could it be local?'

'No, they're all six figures. In fact, these days almost every telephone number you come across is more than four figures, isn't it?'

'I suppose with the area code it has to be, yes.'

'And without that you're sunk. Even a computer would get a brainstorm trying to work out all the possibilities . . . You know, Enrique, RM could be a hell of a lot of other people.'

'Not when the initials appear in Marsh's notebook.'

'But we don't yet know for certain that this Marsh is your Marsh.'

'This proves he is.'

Danois smiled. 'It only proves it if RM is Massier. And you can only put your money on that if you're certain this is your Marsh . . . Which completes the circle!'

'I know I'm right, never mind the proof.'

'But how do I sell that idea to my superiors?'

CHAPTER 18

Alvarez and Danois drove to Guichard's home, where he lived with his parents, at a quarter past seven. It lay on the outskirts of a village and was a small house which need not have appeared as mean in character as it did if a few simple repairs had been carried out and the yard, in which chickens and two pigs roamed at will, had been cleaned up.

Guichard was of medium height, well built, and had a handsome, slightly boyish but not effeminate face. They sat at the kitchen table, Guichard facing Alvarez and Danois, while Guichard's mother, a woman of a nervous disposition, stood in the doorway, asking ridiculous questions, until Danois quietly said they needed to interview her son on their own and would she mind leaving. She left.

'Monsieur Alvarez has some questions for you,' said Danois. 'If you don't answer them quickly and truthfully, you'll spend the next few weeks in the stir.'

Guichard looked fearfully at Alvarez.

'While you were living with Monsieur Marsh, did he ever travel to Mallorca?' Alvarez asked.

Guichard shook his head.

'Did he or didn't he?' demanded Danois with sharp antagonism.

'No, he didn't: never.'

'Did he talk about Mallorca?' Alvarez's attitude remained friendly. The relationship between Marsh and Guichard had not been one he could understand, nevertheless he could accept it without condemnation and therefore had sympathy for someone who had so clearly been hurt by it.

'He never mentioned the place.'

'Then did he ever travel anywhere else?'

'You mean, while I was with him?'

'That's right.'

'He only went away once.'

'Where did he go then?'

'I don't know.'

'So it could have been to Mallorca?'

'I . . . I suppose so.'

'What happened?'

'It was going to be my birthday and when he said he'd be away for it I begged him to take me. I've always wanted to go abroad and we could've had such fun together.'

Danois made a sound of disgust. Guichard flinched.

'He never gave the slightest hint beforehand of where he was going or afterwards where he'd been?'

'No, he didn't. And it wasn't like him to be secretive, but he just wouldn't talk about it.'

'While you lived with him, did many of his friends visit him?'

'Not really. He used to say that most people couldn't understand . . .' He stopped.

'Did you meet anyone by the name of Roger Clarke or did you ever hear his name mentioned?'

'No.'

'How about Peter Short, Simon Allen, or Raymond Massier?'

'I've never heard of any of 'em.'

Alvarez thought for a moment, then looked at Danois. Danois stood. 'If we want you again, we'll know where to find you.'

Guichard stared down at the table and fingered his lips as the two detectives left.

'Well,' said Danois, as they approached Nice along a straight, downhill road, 'what now?'

Alvarez looked at his watch. He spoke sadly. 'I was hoping to get the plane to Barcelona and then a late flight to Mallorca, but it's no good, I've missed it.'

'You're in luck, then.'

'Luck?'

'We'll book you in at a little hotel where I know the owner and they'll give you half rates but make the bill out in full. Then we'll go and liven up the town. If you know where to look, Nice beats Paris any day of the week.'

Neither Nice nor Paris could offer him what he really wanted, he thought sadly.

Dolores hugged him and kissed him on both cheeks several times and generally behaved as if he'd been away for months. After a while, he managed to disengage himself. 'Have there been any messages?'

'None . . . Did you have a good time?'

'I suppose so.'

'What on earth's that mean? What did you do last night?'

'We saw a couple of floor shows at different clubs and drank too much champagne.'

'The next time someone has to go to France, suppose you send me? I'd enjoy it a lot more than you seem to have done.'

He realized that Dolores understood perfectly well why he hadn't enjoyed himself as much as he might have been expected to. 'I'll change and then go along to the post and telephone Palma.'

'You'll be back for lunch?'

'I . . . I'm not certain. It depends what work's waiting.'

She put her hands on her hips. 'Since when has work ever interfered with your lunch?'

'But if there's a lot . . .'

'What you mean is you'll be back if she isn't free. No matter. Don't worry. It doesn't upset me to be treated like a restaurant.'

'Dolores, I . . .' He stopped, accepting that it was useless to try to make her understand. 'Just a moment. I've a present for you.'

She regally accepted a small, elaborately packaged bottle of perfume and kissed him on both cheeks yet again, then went through to the kitchen where she banged the pots and pans about because she loved him like a brother and couldn't bear to see him make such a fool of himself.

He went upstairs and changed into fresh clothes, then left and drove to the guardia post. Once in his room, he telephoned Palma. Salas was there, working on a Sunday!

'Señor, on my arrival in Nice I learned that Señor Marsh died the night before. So we now know that Massier is the murderer.'

'Was Marsh murdered?'

'The circumstances of his death were similar to those in the other cases in that they point to accident. So far, there's no definite proof it wasn't accident, but of course if one considers the previous deaths . . .'

'Can you prove he was the James Marsh who stayed

at Playa del Xima?'

'Yes and no.'

'Alvarez, either you can prove it or you cannot.'

'In Marsh's desk was a notebook he used to jot down notes when telephoning. In this were the initials RM and the numbers nought seven eight two. That has to be Raymond Massier's telephone number. Which means he knew Massier so he is the same Marsh.'

'You can prove that RM refers to the Raymond Massier who was the diving instructor at Playa del Xima?'

'Not yet.'

'Then nothing is certain. Where is the telephone number located?'

'It's very difficult because there are just the four numbers. That means an area code isn't included and without that . . .'

'Has it occurred to you that the figures might not be a telephone number?'

'But I'm certain they are.'

'That inclines me to think that in all probability they are nothing of the sort. Well, what have you done about them?'

'I had a word with the Nice police.'

'What did they say?'

'That it can't be a local number and so there's no way of finding out. But I've asked them to do everything they can to trace Massier. Since he's French, it's likely he's living in France, don't you think?'

Salas didn't bother to answer.

'And also I'll put out a fresh call throughout Spain. We've that photo of him and he can't have changed much in the time. Given the slightest luck, we'll run him to earth.'

'Unfortunately, a very considerable degree of luck is obviously essential if ever you're to bring this case to a successful conclusion,' snapped Salas, before ringing off.

Alvarez left his office and drove down to the port. The bay was at its most beautiful, its colouring dramatic. He gave it hardly a second glance but left his parked car, crossed the road, and walked the short distance to Tracey's flat. The woman downstairs was sitting out on a rocker and she nodded a good-morning and watched him climb the creaking wooden stairs.

He reached the patio and the tension was sharp in his stomach. It was like being twenty again, when the sap ran strong and a man would sell his soul for the joy of a woman's loins . . .

The door was locked. He knew a quick disappointment because he'd been promising himself that, knowing how upset he'd been last time, she'd be there, waiting: he'd step inside to feel the sweetness of her lips against his . . .

Since she wasn't in, she must be on the beach. He turned and walked to the head of the stairs and visually searched as much of the beach as was readily visible, looking for the long, slim figure, in a minimum bikini, that looked so cool and controlled until it was making love . . . He expected to see a waving arm to show she'd seen him, but there was none . . . He went down the stairs.

The woman in the rocker stared at him with beady eyes filled with interest. He was reluctant to say anything that would fuel her gossipy inquisitiveness, but he had to find Tracey as soon as possible. 'I don't suppose you noticed which way the señorita went along the beach this morning?'

The woman rocked. 'She didn't go on the beach this morning,' she finally answered.

'Are you certain of that?'

'Wouldn't say if I wasn't.'

'Have you any idea where she went, then?'

'She didn't go anywhere.'

He tried to remain calm. Nothing would delight her more than to make him lose his temper. 'If she's not in her flat, which she isn't, she must have gone somewhere.'

'Not this morning, she didn't.'

A terrible fear began to freeze his mind. 'What d'you mean?' he asked hoarsely.

'She went yesterday and took all her things with her. She'd paid the rent to the end of the month, so there wasn't anything wrong with that.'

Nothing wrong with it? he thought wildly.

CHAPTER 19

'Uncle,' said Juan, 'will you take me to the bullfight?'

Alvarez, seated on the other side of the dining-table, continued to stare into space.

'Uncle, I want to go to the bullfight.'

'Stop worrying him,' said Dolores.

'But there's never been a bullfight in the village before and I want to see it.'

'There was one here forty years ago,' corrected Jaime.

'Angel says this is the first one ever.'

'Don't contradict your father,' said Dolores.

'But Angel knows and he's never wrong. He says the village was always too poor before.'

'Stuff and nonsense!' Jaime reached out for the bottle of wine and refilled his tumbler. 'I went to one when I was about your age.'

'But Angel says . . .'

'Angel's full of . . .' Just in time, Jaime cut short what he'd been about to say. He turned. 'Here, Enrique, you must remember it?'

Alvarez said listlessly: 'Remember what?'

'When there was last a bullfight in the village.'

'How can he remember that?' asked Dolores. 'When he was young he lived along the coast.'

'But he must have heard about it. A bullfight in the village!'

'Uncle,' said Juan, 'was there a bullfight here years ago?'

'I don't know,' replied Alvarez.

'You don't know anything.'

'Juan!' snapped Dolores.

Juan, muttering mutinously, ate the last of his serving of chocolate layer cake. He stared at the piece left on the serving dish, caught his mother's look, and gloomily came to the conclusion that he was not going to be allowed a second helping.

'Fill your glass up, Enrique,' said Jaime, holding up the bottle of wine.

'Not for me.'

'But you've hardly had any.'

'I've had enough.' Alvarez stood. 'I think I'll go on up.' He left.

Jaime spoke in an undertone to Dolores. 'Is he ill?'

'Must you be quite so stupid?'

'What in God's name have I said now?'

Juan was becoming very bored. 'Can I get up from the table?'

She nodded. 'And you can go and tell Aunty Francisca that it's time Isabel came home.'

'But I wanted to see Bernado and . . .' His mother frowned and he hastily decided that his wants had better be left unstated.

After Juan had gone, Jaime finished the wine in his tumbler, then jerked his head at the ceiling. 'So what d'you think's got into him?'

'You really don't know?'

'If you mean that woman? . . . That's ages ago.'

'And you can't understand how any man's heart can stay broken for longer than a few hours?'

'But it must be . . . nearly a week now. I mean, lose

one, find another. There are always better fish left in the sea than get hooked out.'

'So if I drop down dead tonight, tomorrow you'll find someone better than me?'

'Hell, I wasn't saying anything like that . . .' He trailed off into silence. And as he refilled his glass, he morosely wondered how it was that she invariably manœuvred him into the wrong?

'All the same . . .' she murmured.

'All the same what?'

'Perhaps for once you could be right.'

That she could say such a thing made him vaguely uneasy.

'I wonder if the best way to help him forget about that woman . . .' She spoke the words 'that woman' with bitter scorn. She'd never met the foreigner and didn't even know her name, but she hated her with a sharp passion for having hurt Alvarez. 'D'you know María-Magdalena?'

'Well, of course I know María-Magdalena Vidal,' he said carefully.

'Not her. He's still alive.'

'Who's still alive? What the hell are you talking about?'

'María-Magdalena Belmonte. Her man died last year.'

'Well I know that. I was at the funeral.'

'She's a fine woman.'

'Provided you don't look at her face. He married her before electricity came to everyone.'

'Always the same stupidity! . . . Do you judge whether a cow is a good beast by the look of its face?'

'No, by the size of its udders, and from the looks of hers . . .'

'Be quiet!'

He drained the glass.

'She'll need help looking after her property now.'

'If you're thinking of Enrique, I'd say, forget it.'

'Why?'

'Because he's reached the age where he likes his women young.'

'Men!' she said with contempt.

On Saturday, the last day of July and the penultimate day before the fiesta of Llueso when for almost a week the bars would be open throughout the twenty-four hours and no work would be done by anyone, Dolores — enforcing a rule that was very seldom observed — insisted on having the television switched off at nine, for the sake of her children.

Once the set was off, she looked up from her crocheting and across at Alvarez, who was slumped in one of the armchairs and staring into space, his expression one of sad depression. 'I ran into María-Magdalena this morning. You know, María-Magdalena Belmonte. She was looking a lot better.'

'She needs to, doesn't she?' said Jaime, very resentful at not being allowed to watch the film.

Isabel giggled.

'She's getting over the death of her husband.'

'And he'll be doing his share of rejoicing as well.'

'Will you be quiet,' she said furiously.

Jaime had determined to support Alvarez, but in the face of her anger he decided it was much better to leave a man to fight his own battles.

'I asked her along here. It's nice for her to get out and about after such a sad time.' Her crochet hook flashed backwards and forwards and the intricate floral pattern grew. 'I suggested she came along and had a meal with us tonight since it would make such a nice change for her... I thought she might enjoy the frito mallorquin I made... but she couldn't manage it. But she did say she'd like to come tomorrow if her cousin from Palma doesn't turn up. She'll know by now whether he is or isn't coming. She had the phone put in just before her man died so we could phone her and find out and then I'd know for the cooking.'

'Will she bring me a present?' asked Juan.

'Certainly not.'

'Then let's not phone.'

She allowed her annoyance to surface and immediately made a mistake with the crochet work. It cost her quite an effort to say quietly: 'Enrique, would you like to go and phone for me?' She began to undo her last few stitches.

'What's that?' said Alvarez.

'Would you go and phone her to save me having to do it.'

'Phone who?'

She pulled too hard on the crochet cotton and undid more stitches than she had intended.

Jaime said: 'She wants you to phone María-Magdalena Belmonte, the woman with the large . . .'

'I'll do it, since no one else will,' said Dolores in a thin voice.

Alvarez pulled himself to his feet. 'It's all right, I'll do it. And I might as well turn in afterwards.'

'Come back and have a coñac?' suggested Jaime.

'Not for me.'

Jaime sadly shook his head. When a man ceased to drown his sorrows in drink, he'd lost all zest for living.

Alvarez crossed to the doorway, then stopped. 'Who d'you say I was to ring?'

'María-Magdalena Belmonte,' replied Dolores, exercising a degree of restraint which until now she hadn't known she possessed.

'What's her number?'

'Fourteen twenty.'

Alvarez took one step forward, stopped, turned back. 'What d'you say?'

'Fourteen twenty.'

'No telephone on this island is just four numbers.'
'For Heaven's sake, Enrique, you really must pull yourself together . . .' She nibbled at her lips, then said: 'Of course it isn't. But you know she lives in the village so the number has to start with five three.'

It was amazing, he thought, how one could so easily miss the obvious.

It had always seemed likely that Massier was living either in France or on the island. Alvarez placed the telephone directory on his desk and opened it. The entries began with Palma and then each village was listed separately. He went through each list and noted down the area code, or codes. There was no Raymond Massier living in any area, but such an absence did not carry the significance it might have done in another country. First, the cost of transferring the name in which a telephone was held was so high that many people didn't bother to have the change made, secondly it was a standard complaint that one entry in four was wrong and the other three were suspect.

His twenty-seventh code was 99. As he dialled it, he fleetingly thought that this was not a number one could ever need deliberately to remember. The call was answered by a woman who spoke Mallorquin. 'I want to speak to Señor Raymond Massier,' he said, as he had done twenty-six times already, which had so conditioned him to expect a curt denial that the speaker had ever heard of Massier that he automatically held a pencil ready to strike out 99.

'He's not here,' she said.

He kept the pencil very still. 'When will he be back?'
'Maybe not until late. It's best if you try again tomorrow.'

He thanked her and replaced the receiver. It was odd, but now that he knew he'd run the murderer to earth, he felt no sense of elation. Rather, he was wondering how on earth he was going to explain to Superior Chief Salas how it had taken him until now to locate Massier, even if Massier had obviously never bothered to apply for either a residencia or a permanencia?

CHAPTER 20

The mountain backbone of the island tended, on its south side, to peter out into hills before these too gently subsided into the central plain. Among the hills, particularly in the centre, were a number of valleys, some large, some small. Massier lived in one of the smallest—once it had been known as the lost valley. There was only one access track to it and this led through steep cliffs which at one stage came within twelve metres of each other: a torrente, dry throughout the spring, summer, and autumn, occasionally a roaring, dangerous torrential river in the winter, ran alongside the track.

The floor of the valley was almost level, except for a topped sugar-loaf mound in the middle: on this mound was a two hundred year old rock-built farmhouse, with walls more than a metre thick, small windows, and a heavy wooden front door with a cat hole. Beyond the house were three large, rock-built barns, once used for storing all the food necessary to keep the farmer, his family, and his animals, until the next harvest. Both house and barns had been restored and modernized, but this had been done with such sympathetic care that the fact was not immediately apparent: only when close did one notice that the faces of some of the rocks in the walls were of a different shade from the rest and that the limestone blocks above the windows were unscarred by weather. What was immediately obvious, however, was the fact that no farmer now lived there. Instead of crops reaching up to the house, there was a garden right round.

The track into the valley had been metalled and Alvarez was able to drive up to a pair of gates from which stretched a heavy chain-link fence surrounding the garden, topped with three strands of barbed wire. There was a notice on the right-hand gate, in French and Spanish: it advised callers that the property was guarded by a dog and therefore to ring the bell. He rang the bell. Immediately a dog began to bark with deep, fierce intensity.

A woman, dressed in a cotton frock over which was an apron, stepped out of a doorway to the side of the house. 'You can come in,' she shouted. 'The dog's locked up.'

He opened the right-hand gate and went inside. The garden was filled with colour which ranged from the blues of hydrangeas to the delicate pink trumpets of a datura tree.

As his shoes crunched on the stone-chips surface of the drive, the dog's barks redoubled in volume until the woman shouted at it to shut up and then it lapsed into silence. He came up to where the woman stood and saw, chained to a kennel, a huge black dog, as hairy as a yak, which was watching him with lips drawn back to disclose a lethal set of fangs.

He pointed at the dog, an act which immediately provoked a rising growl. 'I'm glad that's tied up!'

'You need to be,' she replied. 'He can be vicious to someone he doesn't know . . . What d'you want?'

'Inspector Alvarez, Cuerpo General de Policia.'

She shielded her eyes from the fierce sun with her right hand as she studied him. 'Enrique Alvarez from Llueso? . . . Remember me? Josephina Zimmerman, though I was Herrera Vila when we last saw each other.'

'Of course,' he said, trying to equate this middle-aged, stocky woman with a heavily lined face with a girl as fresh and as beautiful as a rosebud who had lived in the village.

'How have things been?'

'There've been troubles. I married a foreigner and when I had my boy and was ill, he left me.'

'I'm sorry to hear that.' The foreigners plundered everything, he thought bitterly.

She shrugged her shoulders. She belonged, as did he, to the last generation of islanders which had been born into poverty and who, in consequence, had never believed that the world owed them, or would provide them with, a smooth passage through life. 'I work here for the señor and he pays. And my son is doing very well at school in his first year. They say he's clever.'

'That's wonderful to hear. And how's your brother who also moved away?'

'We don't see each other. He could never accept me marrying a foreigner.'

Years of silence, he thought, just because of that. Yet now the youngsters had little bastards and no one seemed to think twice about it. 'Is the señor in?'

She nodded. 'He doesn't go out unless he has to, like yesterday, since she left.'

'She?'

'Another foreigner and much younger than him, but she was nice.' Her tone suggested the combination was unusual. 'Always full of fun.'

'When did she leave him?'

'Maybe a week ago: maybe a little more.'

'D'you know why?'

'Why?' She shrugged her shoulders. 'Who can know why? One day she was as always, the next she wasn't here and he told me she'd left him. Perhaps she suddenly understood that it was all too difficult. There's only ever trouble when an old man knows a young woman.'

He winced.

A bell sounded inside the house.

'That's him calling. I must go and see what he wants.'

'Tell him I want a word with him.'

'All right. You'd best come on into the kitchen to wait.'

The kitchen was large and very well equipped, yet it still managed to be in keeping with the beamed ceiling and the roughly faced walls. If only more old farmhouses had been restored with such loving care, he thought, remembering Ca Na Rostra.

She was gone a couple of minutes and when she returned she said: 'The señor's not feeling well and can't see you.'

'He's got to see me.'

She became uneasy.

'He's not in bed, is he?'

She shook her head.

'Then take me through to wherever he is.'

She hesitated, then led the way out of the kitchen, through the hall, under an archway which supported stone stairs, and into the high-ceilinged sitting-room, which had a second floor, or primitive gallery, at the far end. 'Señor, the detective says he must speak to you . . .'

'I told you to tell him I'm too ill,' Massier shouted, his Spanish fluent but his accent heavy.

Alvarez stepped forward to come into view. Massier looked considerably older than he had in the photograph. His face was lined, his hair had receded and become grey, and the suggestion of hard physical condition had given way to one of flabbiness.

'Why d'you let him in . . .' he began wildly.

'I insisted,' said Alvarez.

Massier slumped back into the high wing chair. Josephina looked from one man to the other, then said: 'Do you wish for coffee, señor?'

He shook his head.

Alvarez said: 'Bring him a coñac.'

She hurried out of the room.

Alvarez moved to a second chair and sat. 'Your name

is Raymond Massier?'

'What if it is?' Massier's voice was deep and husky, like that of a man who smoked too much.

'You once worked as an instructor in scuba-diving at Playa del Xima?'

'No.'

Alvarez brought a print of the photograph from the breast pocket of his shirt. He stood, crossed the carpeted floor, and held the photo out.

'I tell you . . .'

'And I tell you that I can drive you to Playa del Xima and find half a dozen people, including Garcia, who'll identify you immediately.'

Massier shivered.

'You see the other two men?'

'Well?'

'Do you remember their names?'

'No.'

'One was Roger Clarke and the other was Simon Allen.'

'What . . . what d'you want?'

Josephina returned, carrying a tray on which were two glasses, a bottle, a soda syphon, and an insulated ice container. She put the tray down on a table, stared uneasily at them, then left, without having spoken.

Alvarez returned the photo to his shirt pocket and went over to the table. He poured out two brandies, handed one glass to Massier, returned to his chair. 'There were five of you and Loco Llobera. Llobera told you where the Marqués de Orlocas's boat had sunk and you dived and found the wreck. And even though it was nearly fifty years before, the jewels and the gold plate were still in the wreck and you salvaged them.

'Llobera wasn't as completely stupid as people thought him, but neither was he even halfway to being normal. So once he'd led you to the fortune, he had to be eliminated in case he might start boasting about how he'd got his own back on the Marqués's family. You murdered him by getting him drunk and then pushing him over the cliffs at Setray.'

'No.'

'Yes,' he contradicted harshly. 'And that's when you made your first mistake. You gave him a bottle of cognac, from France, instead of a bottle of coñac, from Spain, to make certain he got drunk.'

'I don't know what you're talking about.' Sweat had gathered on Massier's face and it was beginning to slide down his cheeks and nose.

'Did the other four know that Llobera had died?'

'I swear I didn't know him or anything about him.'

'Obviously they didn't. Which is understandable. If they had learned that, they might have begun to realize what you intended to do when you reckoned it was safe to do it.'

Massier stumbled to his feet and went across to pour himself out a second and much larger drink.

'You waited three years before you decided it was the right time to move. That must have seemed a very long three years as you watched the other four all spending furiously. But at least you'd managed to persuade them that it would be the height of folly to sell all the jewels and plate at once, so there'd been no general distribution and the bulk of the treasure—now worth God knows how many times more than it had been when it went to the bottom of the sea—was intact so that you knew that when you'd murdered everyone else there'd still be a fortune waiting for you.

'This year, you started. You murdered Clarke, Allen Short, and Marsh. And when you murdered Marsh by getting him drunk and then pushing him out of the window, you believed you'd finally secured everything for yourself . . . Where are the jewels and gold plate?'

Massier, who'd remained standing by the table,

drained his glass and then refilled it with shaking hands. He drank greedily.

'Where are they?'

'I don't know anything,' he croaked.

'Are they on this island?'

'I don't know what you're talking about.'

Alvarez sighed. 'Sit down.'

Moving like a sleepwalker, Massier returned to his chair.

'When did you first come to this island?'

'About . . . eight years ago.'

'Did you come here to live?'

He shook his head.

'What then?'

'Just for the summer, to teach diving.'

'What happened in the winter?'

'I returned to France.'

'Are you married?'

He hesitated, then nodded.

'Where's your wife now?'

'I don't know.'

'When did she leave you?'

'Five years ago.'

'Was she fed up with your beachcombing way of life?'

He didn't answer.

'Whereabouts did you live in France?'

'In Paris.'

'Did you own the place you lived in?'

'No.'

'Why not?'

'I . . . couldn't afford to.'

'D'you own this house?'

'Yes.'

'How much did it cost to buy and restore?'

Incredibly, he had failed to realize where the previous questions had been leading. He stared at Alvarez, even more frightened than before.

'Fifty million would be a conservative estimate, wouldn't it? Where did that sort of money come from? And where does the money come from to run the house and employ Josephina and the gardener?'

'I . . . I won it.'

'On what?'

'The lottery.'

'When?'

'Three years ago.'

'How many millions did you win?'

'I . . . I don't remember exactly.'

'I'd have thought that that sort of memory would accompany one to the grave. But it must have been a lot more than fifty million. At which bank did you encash the ticket?'

He realized that to give any answer would be merely to make it that much more easy to prove he was lying.

'Where were you on Friday, the twenty-third of last month?'

'Why d'you ask?'

'It's when Señor James Marsh was murdered in the village of Pelonette, near Nice.'

'I haven't left the island in months.'

'Can you prove that?'

'Ask Josephina.'

'Does she work here over the weekends?'

He shook his head.

'So she can never vouch for you on a Saturday or Sunday . . . You flew to Nice on Friday night, after she'd finished here, and you returned some time Saturday. Passports are seldom stamped at borders these days, so you thought you were safe.'

'I swear to God I haven't left the island in months.'

'You hold God that lightly?'

'Then ask . . . ask Marion.'

'Who?'

His expression crumpled.

'Who's Marion?'

'She . . . she used to live here.'

'When did she leave?'

'Nine days ago,' he said in a whisper.

'Why did she leave? Because she'd begun to suspect the truth about your visit to France?'

'No.'

'Where is she now?'

'I . . . I don't know.'

Alvarez finished his drink, then stood. 'I want your passport.'

Massier looked up, his expression pleading. 'If I . . .' he swallowed heavily.

'Well?'

'The jewels and gold . . . What happens to them?'

'When they are positively identified? They'll be returned to their legal owner, the Marqués de Orlocas's daughter.'

'Couldn't . . .' He stopped. His expression changed. 'I don't know anything about them,' he said vehemently.

'Your passport, please. And you will make no attempt to leave this island until further inquiries have been carried out.'

Massier came to his feet and then stumbled out of the room.

CHAPTER 21

Dolores had just poured out a second bowlful of cocoa for Alvarez when the phone rang. She showed no inclination to go and answer the call so he regretfully came to his feet and went through.

One of the guards at the post said: 'There's a message

come in for you from Señora Josephina Zimmerman. She says she's just arrived at Señor Massier's house and he's shot himself and what's she to do?'

'Is he dead?'

'She says he must have been dead for some hours.'

In this heat, Alvarez thought grimly, the ravages of death soon became very apparent. It had not happened in his department, yet it was his case and there could be no doubt that Salas (to whom it must be reported) would direct him to carry out the investigation. 'Look, do me a favour, will you? Get on to the police doctor for the Treller department and ask him . . .'

'Sorry, mate, I've too much to do as it is,' said the guard, before replacing the receiver.

Alvarez swore, thought, then returned to the kitchen. 'I've got to get moving right away.'

'You're not going anywhere until you've finished the cocoa and ensaimada,' corrected Dolores. 'Not when I took all the trouble to go out early to the baker to get the ensaimada for you . . . Anyway, what's happened?'

'A man's committed suicide. Thankfully.'

'Thankfully?' she repeated, shocked.

'Now, everything's over and done with.' He sat on a stool at the small kitchen table.

'But suicide, Enrique?'

'There are times when I really can't see it as a sin, whatever the priests say. If it's kinder to everyone, including himself, how can it be so wrong?'

She shook her head. There were times when she completely failed to understand him.

He unwound part of the ensaimada and dunked it in the cocoa, then ate. Just over three years ago, there had been five men whose lives had been very ordinary. Then a sixth man, a tragic fool, had shown them a vision of riches beyond their wildest dreams and because men always longed for what they normally could only dream about, they'd pursued those riches without any thought to the cost. The cost had proved to be tragically high. Four murders and a suicide . . .

Massier lay on the floor of the small room, beyond the sitting-room, which Josephina referred to as the library, even though there were no shelves of books, but only a few paperbacks in a metal-framed bookcase.

The gun was a 9mm Lebel automatic and he'd put the muzzle against his right temple and pulled the trigger. There was a thin ring around the entry wound, due to pressure of the soiled muzzle, the skin was split and scorched, and the muzzle area alone was speckled with particles of partly burned powder. He'd been sitting on a chair behind the desk and at the moment of death an involuntary movement had thrown him off this on to the ground. His right arm was outstretched, his left was by his side: the automatic lay between his body and his right arm. The ejected cartridge case was three metres away. There was surprisingly little blood. His eyes were partially open and his lips were parted to show his upper teeth. Already, flies were bothering his corpse.

Alvarez crossed to the single window and looked out. The beauty of the enclosed valley, surrounded by mountains, increased the ugliness of the death behind him. Why, he wondered bitterly, did man forever destroy . . .

He left the library and went through to the sitting-room, where he found Josephina. 'The doctor should be here soon and then the body can be moved . . . D'you know if there's a safe in the house?'

She nodded. 'There's one in the library: behind one of the paintings on the wall.' She hesitated, then said worriedly: 'I know only about it because I went in there one day and he'd left it open.'

He said easily: 'D'you think I could imagine there'd be any other reason?'

She was relieved and grateful for this implicit testimony to her honesty.

He returned to the library. There were three coloured prints of roses hanging on the walls and the last one he checked proved to be concealing the safe. As had happened not long before in the case, he searched for the key and this time found it almost immediately, in the top right-hand drawer of the desk. He opened the safe, which was much larger than the size of the door suggested. There were a few pieces of personal jewellery — cuff-links, tiepins, and dress studs — some papers which included the escrituras of house and land, and nearly five hundred thousand pesetas and six thousand Swiss francs in notes. But no collection of stolen jewellery and gold plate.

He relocked the safe and replaced the key in the desk drawer. Massier must surely have recovered the four shares of the men he'd murdered, so where was this fortune? Was there so much that it wouldn't fit into the safe? But even the most valuable jewellery would pack into a relatively small space and surely there wouldn't have been so much gold plate that it would have overflowed this large safe? And even if this was wrong and there had been that much, wouldn't he have kept the jewellery in the safe, as being the more valuable, and the gold somewhere else?

Josephina was in the kitchen. 'If the señor had something valuable,' he asked, 'but he didn't want it in the safe, can you think where he might have kept it?'

The question clearly bewildered her.

'What about one of the outbuildings?' he suggested.

'He used the first one for a garage and there's some wood and tools in the second one, otherwise they're empty.'

'How much land did he own?'

'Just the garden. When he bought the house he was

offered the farmland as well, but he said he didn't want it.'

The house and the outbuildings would have to be searched from top to bottom: the garden would have to be checked with a metal detector and, if necessary, dug over: the banks would have to be asked about safe-deposits . . .

She interrupted his thoughts. 'What's the best thing for me to do now?'

'I'd say you might as well pack up and go home. That is, after you've told me where you live in case I need some more help.'

'I'll do that, then. I suppose . . . I suppose it's happened because of you coming here yesterday?'

'I'm afraid so.'

'What was the trouble?'

'He'd been mixed up in something nasty.'

'I'd never have thought it of him. You just can't tell these days, can you?'

She gave him her address, then began to leave but stopped at the door and turned back. 'What's to happen about the dog?'

'How d'you mean?'

'Well, feeding it.'

'I hadn't thought about that . . . Can you come in each day until I can find out exactly what's what? Can't say I'd like the idea of trying to cope with it.'

'He's all right if he knows you.'

'That's just as well or from the looks of him you wouldn't have got very far past the gates this morning.'

'There'd have been no trouble. He was still chained up. The señor must have forgotten to turn him loose. Wasn't thinking straight, knowing what he was going to do.'

What thoughts did go through a man's mind when he knew he was going to kill himself? Alvarez wondered.

Alvarez telephoned Palma at 9.17 that evening.

'Have you checked the garden?' demanded Salas.

'Yes, señor. We used a metal detector and had several responses, but none of them proved significant. The gardener says it would be impossible for anything of any size to be buried anywhere in the garden without his knowing.'

'I don't suppose you've thought to check with the banks if he's deposited the stuff in one of their strong-rooms?'

'Indeed, yes.'

'You have!'

'He hasn't made such a deposit.'

'Then it has to be hidden somewhere about the house or the outbuildings and you've failed to find it.'

'I've had five men searching every nook and cranny. I'll swear it's not anywhere around.'

'Then that just leaves somewhere abroad.'

'Yes, señor. I think that originally they took everything abroad so there could never be the possibility of their recovery of the fortune coming to light by accident. Since then, they've just been encashing what they immediately needed.'

'Then it'll be deposited somewhere totally secure, probably a bank's strong-room. Among Massier's papers there must be a receipt for the deposit.'

'There isn't.'

'Check again, more thoroughly.'

'I assure you, señor, if there were such a receipt, I would have found it. And if you remember, we've not come across such a receipt with any of the other dead men.'

'Then exactly how d'you propose to locate the jewellery and gold?'

'At the moment,' he confessed, 'I've no idea.'

'You do realize, do you, that until they are returned to the daughter of the Marqués de Orlocas, the case cannot be considered closed?'

'I suppose it can't.'

'There's no suppose about it. You'd better start thinking and find out where it is.'

Alvarez sighed. Just for once, Salas might have been generous enough to have credited him with successfully solving a case.

CHAPTER 22

The next morning Alvarez left the guardia post at 12.47 and drove home, taking a short cut up a one-way street, travelling the wrong way. His mind was fixed on the question which had been exercising it so bitterly. The jewellery and gold plate were not hidden in Massier's house, outbuildings, or garden, and they hadn't been deposited in any bank in Spain. So they must be hidden abroad. Where abroad? There were no leads left to follow and the last man who'd known the truth had shot himself . . .

Parked outside his house was a newly registered Seat. Probably one of Dolores's friends, he thought, who'd just bought a new car and was showing it off. He crossed the pavement and entered the house. The transition from harsh sunlight to dim interior was so great that although he was immediately aware someone was in the front room, it took him a second to identify her. 'Tracey!' he said thickly.

Her expression was uneasy.

'I knew you'd come back, my darling.' He took a step forward, his arms held out.

'No,' she said sharply. 'Oh God, Enrique, why do you have to make it even more difficult for me?'

He dropped his arms to his side. 'What d'you mean?'

'I discovered I couldn't leave without saying goodbye to you.'

'Leave?'

'I'm flying to England tomorrow morning and on home to New Zealand.'

'Then why come here?' he demanded, his voice filled with aching pain.

'I've just said: I had to say goodbye . . . I was going to leave, just like that, but I was in my hotel room in Palma and suddenly knew I had to come here and say goodbye. We've got to part friends.'

'Friends? After all that's happened, you speak just in terms of friendship?'

'Please try to understand.'

'Why? So that you can have a peaceful conscience?'

'That's a horrid thing to say . . . Why won't you try to understand?'

'Because I love you.'

'And I loved you.'

'Loved. Not love.'

'It could never have lasted.'

'Why couldn't it?'

'Because . . .' She desperately searched for words. 'I told you, right at the beginning, I'm selfish. I'm not like Marion, who never stops thinking of other people. I'm totally selfish. I can't help it. But I was honest about it, wasn't I?'

'Then when we first made love and for me the world had turned into light, you were thinking of how soon you'd go away and leave me in darkness?'

'It wasn't like that at all.'

'But you knew even then that you'd end it?'

'I . . . I didn't think that way.'

'Then you must have believed it would last. What changed your mind? Did you suddenly realize I'm so much older than you?'

'That's nothing to do with it. You're twisting what I say.'

'How can I twist words I don't understand?'

'You won't understand. Your pride's hurt and you're trying to get your own back on me.'

'Can you really think I would be like that?'

She slowly shook her head. 'No, not you. Oh, Christ, I hate myself! But can't you see, it's because it was so wonderful that I had to come here now and be honest for . . .' She stopped.

'Were you going to say, for once?'

'Yes.'

'Then don't you see, you love me more than you've ever loved anyone else? Let's start again. We'll picnic on Barrats Hill. We'll explore all the beautiful, hidden parts of the island. I'll take you to—'

'Stop it. I'm leaving tomorrow.'

'Why?'

'Because . . . because . . . I shouldn't have come here,' she said wildly. 'Goodbye, Enrique. If only . . .' She came forward and seemed to be going to kiss him, but then just rested her fingers on his cheek for a second. She turned, crossed to the door, and went out.

After a moment, he ran across and followed her into the blinding sunshine. She was behind the wheel of the car and through the open window he could see her curly, copper-coloured hair that had tickled his face, her generous lips which had pressed so warm and moist on his . . .

She drove away, without once looking back. He returned into the house.

Supper, which might have been a sad meal, was enlivened by the excited chatter of Juan and Isabel. Had the adults heard? The sports centre, with gymnasium, indoor basketball pitch, and swimming pool, proposed for so many years it had become a joke, was actually going to be built! Three men had been seen surveying the site. One of them had said that by next summer it would be possible to go and swim . . .

'Here, have some more wine,' said Jaime, and he pushed the bottle across the table.

Alvarez refilled his glass. He drank. The alcohol was beginning to build a layer between him and the world and for that he was grateful. He even found his thoughts returning to the case. So typical of Salas to refuse to credit him with solving the case just because he couldn't do the impossible and recover the treasure . . . Funny, but something Tracey had said earlier seemed to be of some significance . . . But that was impossible because she'd been trying to make him understand something that it was impossible for him to understand . . . More impossibities . . .

'Enrique, are you feeling all right?' Dolores asked, her tone very worried.

'Uncle's drunk too much,' said Juan.

'How dare you!' snapped Dolores as she brought her right arm round and boxed him on his ear. He'd been threatened with corporal punishment often enough, but so seldom had he actually been hit that it was several seconds before he overcame the shock sufficiently to start bawling. The moment he did so, Dolores became frightened she'd hit him far harder than she'd intended . . .

'Sometimes,' said Jaime, as Dorlores, Juan, and Isabel, consoling each other, left the dining-room, 'I wonder what they mean by the joys of a family . . . Here, now we've got some peace, let's have a coñac?'

'I don't think I'd better drink any more.'

'Why not? You're not going anywhere, are you?' Immediately he'd spoken, Jaime realized that this was perhaps not the most tactful remark he could have made and he hastily stood and crossed to the sideboard where he poured out two large brandies.

As Alvarez drank, the confusion in his mind grew, but then, as abruptly as if a curtain had been drawn, he remembered Tracey saying: 'I'm selfish. I'm not like

Marion, who never stops thinking of other people.' She'd never mentioned a Marion before. Could this be the same Marion who'd been with Massier up until a few days before his suicide? But Josephina had said that one day Marion had appeared to love Massier as much as ever, the next he'd told her she'd left him. That was the action of a selfish woman. Yet if the two Marions were one and the same person, Tracey had implied that she was the very opposite to selfish . . .'

'. . . so what d'you think, Enrique?'

'I think I've got to move,' he answered thickly.

'Going to be sick?'

'Got to make a telephone call.'

'Now?'

'Is she selfish? I've got to know.'

Poor old sod, thought Jaime. But that's what happened when you were middle-aged and fell for a young bit of skirt. Not that he mightn't have done the same, judging from Dolores's description of the woman. All sex and nothing more. But what more did any man want?

By concentrating very carefully, Alvarez managed to reach the telephone. He tried to remember the number of the guardia post, but all he could recall was one which, after due deliberation, he decided was his own. He picked up the book in which frequently used numbers were entered, but had great difficulty in working out under what letter the guardia post was listed . . .

'What on earth are you doing?' Dolores asked.

'Try . . . trying to . . . to phone the post.'

'If you've any sense left you'll wait until tomorrow.'

He shook his head. 'Must . . . must phone now.'

'Then give me the book.' She read the number, dialled it, then handed the receiver across.

The call was answered.

'I want . . . I want . . .' began Alvarez.

'Who the hell's that?'

'Inspector Alvarez . . .'
'Pissed as usual, from the sound of it.'
'Ring Palma and tell 'em . . . tell 'em . . .'
'All right, tell 'em what?'
He took a deep breath and concentrated very hard. 'They must . . . find out which hotel Señorita Tracey Newcombe is staying . . . Very urgent . . . Flying away in the morning. Going away.'
'But not as far gone as you are!'
He tried to put the receiver down, but missed. Dolores took it from him. 'Go up to bed,' she said softly.
He staggered up to his room and collapsed on the bed. The world spun away into darkness.

He awakened by the ringing of the telephone. A moment later, Dolores called up: 'Enrique, are you awake?'
He groaned.
There was a sharp knock on the door of the bedroom. 'Are you up?' The door opened and she looked in. 'How are you feeling?'
'Terrible.'
'Then you'd better stay where you are. That was the post ringing to say Palma has discovered which hotel the woman is staying in.'
'Where?'
'It doesn't matter right now. By far the best thing for you is to stay in bed . . .'
'What's the name of the hotel?'
She wanted to tell him to forget the woman once and for all, but experience had taught her that it would be no good. 'The Alicante. I've made a note of the number.'
'What's the time now?'
'It's nine-fifteen.'
He sat up abruptly, then groaned as his head throbbed more violently. 'I must talk before she goes.'
As she left, she sent a brief prayer skywards that by the

time he phoned, the woman would already have boarded the plane and flown out.

He dressed, then went downstairs and along to the telephone. He dialled the number which Dolores had written on the pad. When the connection was made, he asked to speak to Señorita Newcombe.

After a moment, Tracey said: 'Yes?'

'It's Enrique.'

'Why have you phoned? Why couldn't you have left it? I told you . . .'

'Who's Marion?'

'What?'

'Yesterday you said you weren't like Marion. Who is she?'

'Are you ringing about her?'

'Yes.'

'I thought . . .' She stopped.

'Who is Marion?'

'I met her in Puerto Llueso one day: she's a fellow New Zealander.'

'Who lived with a Frenchman called Raymond Massier?'

'Yes. Why d'you want to know?'

'When you said to me you weren't like her, what exactly were you implying?'

'Just . . . just that we're very different kinds of people.'

'Does that mean that she was happy to go on living with a man a lot older than herself?'

'Enrique, please don't go on like this.'

'Is that what you meant?'

'I . . . perhaps,' she said, in little more than a whisper.

'D'you know why she left Massier?'

'I didn't know she had . . . Though I do remember she said she might have to.'

'Why was she going to have to?'

'Because he said she would.'

'Because he was afraid for her or for himself?'
'I don't know. I wasn't interested. It's just that she was in a state one day and wanted to talk to someone. And because we came from the same country, she talked to me.'
'Did she say anything else?'
'Only that if she did have to go he'd give her enough money to make certain she could wait for him.'
'Where is she now?'
'But I can't know that . . . Enrique, I swear it wasn't just the difference in our ages. The way of life's so different out here. And I became homesick . . .'
He interrupted her. 'Goodbye, Tracey, and good luck.'
'Please tell me you understand . . .'
He put the receiver down and stared unseeingly at the far wall. Massier had been frightened that something would happen either to Marion or himself. Why?

CHAPTER 23

As Alvarez sat on his bed, he heard the distant chime of one of the church clocks striking the half-hour. There were only two reasons why Massier would have been frightened. First, because he feared the police were hot on his heels. But until the visit on Monday, he could not have had the slightest idea that the police had connected together the deaths of the four men, let alone that they had decided that those deaths had been murder and that he, as the surviving member, was obviously the murderer. Second, that he was in fear of his own life. But why should he have been unless the murderer was after him? And, by definition, that was ridiculous since he was the murderer . . .

But the dog had been chained up when Josephina arrived on the morning of Massier's death, when normally it had been left loose all night to guard the house. The obvious explanation for this was that when a man intended to commit suicide he didn't concern himself with routine or worry about his house being broken into. But it was worth remembering that it was easy to divert even a well-trained guard dog if one had a bitch on heat . . . Marion hadn't wanted to leave Massier: he hadn't wanted her to go. Yet he had sent her away. The fact that Massier's telephone number had been jotted down in Marsh's notebook meant they'd been in communication. Just before Marion had left, had Massier telephoned Marsh, to learn that he'd died in an 'accident'? And did Massier then connect this with Allen's 'accidental' drowning, a report of which had been in the paper? . . . There'd been a one-franc piece in the car in which Clarke had crashed; an empty bottle of French cognac at the point from which Llobera had 'fallen' down the cliff; a French Lebel automatic had killed Massier. Meaningless coincidences? Or subtle clues, designed to lead the police on to believing, should they ever suspect murder, that the murderer had been French . . . ?

Yet to suppose that Massier had not committed suicide but had been murdered was to spit at logic. If the murders were connected, and they were, then there had to be a motive common to all of them: this was the jewellery and gold which had been salvaged from the wreck of the Marqués de Orlocas's boat. Since no word that this had been recovered had ever leaked out, it was safe to say that no one but those who'd taken part in the salvage knew what had happened. So only one of the five could have had a motive for killing the other four. Yet if Massier had been murdered, all five had been murdered by a sixth person. But there was no sixth person . . .

Massier's death had to be suicide. But that was to return to the questions, of whom had he been frightened, why was the dog chained up, and was a man clever enough to make four murders appear to be accidents likely to be stupid enough to leave behind obvious clues which pointed directly at himself?

'Alvarez,' said Salas over the telephone, 'do you think you're completely sane?'
'I think so, señor,' he replied.
'Then how do you explain this call? You've very carefully and at great length detailed all the reasons why Massier *must* have committed suicide, only to carry on and tell me you believe he may have been murdered.'
'It's difficult . . .'
'Obviously. So just concentrate on finding the jewellery and the gold plate.'

Alvarez leaned down and opened the bottom right-hand drawer of his desk. He brought out the bottle of brandy and a glass. He had but recently sworn off alcohol, true, but an emergency was an emergency . . .

He'd proved to his own satisfaction that the major part of the treasure must still be intact. Yet if intact, it would be held somewhere very secure, where no unauthorized person, either by chance or design, could gain access and this indicated some form of safe-deposit abroad. Banks offered this facility as did a growing number of commercial security firms.

All five men would have demanded to be present whenever the jewellery and gold were taken out of deposit — only then could each one of them be satisfied that he wasn't being cheated. But it was obvious from the fact of the murders that fewer than five had the right of withdrawal. In other words, the arrangement was in the form of a tontine. Survivor takes all.

All Spanish banks and safe-deposits had been checked and it was as certain as it could be that the fortune hadn't been lodged in any of them. That made sense. Get everything right out of the country immediately. So it was abroad. The country in which it had been stored must be within quick and easy reach of where all the members of the tontine lived. So that really meant western Europe. But just how many countries did that signify? Portugal, France, Germany, United Kingdom, Switzerland, Austria, Italy, Holland, Belgium, Luxembourg, Liechtenstein . . .

He struggled to work out why the name of Liechtenstein should in this context hold some special significance. And then he remembered Vera Allen's never-ending complaints, one of which had been that her husband wouldn't take her on a short trip to Liechtenstein. And Tracey had mentioned a trip Clarke had made abroad on which he'd refused to take her. And Guichard had resented being left behind by Marsh . . .

Liechtenstein. He knew so little about the country that it was only with difficulty he placed it as lying between Austria and Switzerland. But it was common knowledge that it had some of the securest banking laws in the world, in some respects more secure than in Switzerland, and that therefore it offered a haven for 'dirty' money or 'dirty' deposits. So a request to the police authorities there for their help in identifying a deposit made some three years before was virtually doomed to refusal. No blanket request of this nature was ever accepted. The only possible way in which cooperation might be gained would be to identify the deposit and prove that the contents had been criminally obtained.

It was a straightforward and easy task to prove that the contents had been criminally obtained and a detailed description of the jewellery and gold plate could almost certainly be obtained from the Marqués de Orlocas's daughter. But to identify the deposit when there might be hundreds in one bank and dozens of banks and safe-deposit stores . . .

There was nothing to go on, not even a bank name.

How could any identification be made? Yet wasn't there significance in the fact that the murders of Clarke, Short, Allen, and Marsh, (there was no need at this point to twist one's mind into a hundred knots over Massier's death) had taken place so close together in time, when it would have been far more sensible from the murderer's point of view to space them out, thus decreasing the chances of anyone's connecting them? It suggested an overwhelming need to hurry. Presumably brought about by a decision to withdraw all the remaining jewellery and plate and sell it. (When a man started to live luxuriously, his ambitions increased until he wanted to live still more luxuriously. It would prove increasingly irksome to know that this was quite possible if only . . . Three years had passed since the treasure had been recovered. Surely it was safe now to put the bulk of it on the market?) The murderer had had to move quickly if he were to secure the entire fortune for himself before the date of withdrawal.

What date? Tracey had known Clarke to make only one trip. Guichard had been with Marsh for over a year and Marsh had made only the one trip. Vera Allen, who'd lived on the island for just under three years, had referred to her husband's trips. All this suggested that only one visit to make a withdrawal had taken place each year and this sounded reasonable because the tontine would have been drawn up with rigid rules to prevent any cheating. What chance was there of determining the date when no date of any significance had ever been mentioned or found in writing? . . . None.

He slumped back in the chair, lifted his glass, and drained it. What did he have now? A murderer, when there could be no murderer, and a date which couldn't be determined . . .

And then he remembered that Guichard's resentment at being left behind in the house in Pelonette had been exacerbated by the fact that Marsh was going to be away for his birthday . . . He'd get on to Danois by phone and ask him to find out the date of Guichard's birthday. And then he'd try to explain his reasoning to Salas and persuade the superior chief that, armed with a definite date and proof that the fortune had been illegally obtained, there might be a chance of persuading the Liechtenstein authorities to cooperate . . .

Alvarez, already breathless because of the altitude, stepped out of the Hotel Rheineck and began to walk up the steep Brunnenstrasse. He stopped in front of a philatelic shop and studied several sheets of stamps, the country's most profitable export. He must buy some sets for Juan, who'd begun collecting the previous year. That was, if he had any money left at the end of his stay. The brandy he'd had last night at the hotel had cost so much that when he'd translated the Swiss francs into pesetas he'd almost choked.

He walked on, crossing a road when the traffic was halted by lights and shivering as the icy wind dug through his lightweight clothing — winter already? Back home, it would be boiling hot. He reached the far pavement and the buildings once more provided some cover from the wind.

He arrived at the ten-storey concrete and glass building and went in. A pink-cheeked man in a formal black coat was on duty in the foyer and he asked a question in German. Alvarez answered in French and then, seeing that he was not being understood, switched to English. The pink-cheeked man wished him good morning and escorted him to a lift where he indicated the button for the tenth floor.

At the tenth floor a secretary was waiting. Tall, slim, very attractive, her formal smile offered nothing. As he followed her along the corridor, he reflected that the further away from the Mediterranean one got, the colder became both the weather and the women.

They went through one room, clearly the secretary's, into another beyond. Larger, and almost luxuriously furnished, its most noticeable feature was a sculpture on a plinth, which was all curves and had the property of completely changing its form as the angle of viewing altered.

There were three men in the room. Behind the desk was the eldest: tall, with a finely boned face that had an air of unemotional authority, he was dressed in a pinstriped suit of expensive tailoring. 'Herr Alvarez,' said the secretary, 'may I present Herr Bahr.'

Bahr walked round the desk and shook hands with Continental seriousness. 'I trust you had a pleasant journey,' he said in Spanish.

'Thank you, señor, yes I did.'

'And the hotel is satisfactory?'

'It's very comfortable.'

'That is good.' He half turned and said to the secretary: 'Thank you, Helga.'

She left.

'Herr Alvarez, do you speak German?'

'I'm afraid only English and French.'

'You speak English—excellent. I asked Herr Arendt to be present to translate, but that will not now be necessary since Commissioner Goppel speaks English. Please excuse me one moment.' He spoke rapidly to the younger of the two men, who inclined his head in what was half-way between a nod and a brief bow, then marched out of the room.

'Such a serious young man,' said Bahr, 'but an excellent interpreter. His mother was Polish and, as they say, anyone who can speak Polish finds no difficulty in speaking a dozen other languages . . . Now, let me introduce you to Commissioner Goppel, head of the Security Corps.'

Goppel was dressed in the khaki coloured jacket, dark

trousers with coloured stripe, black tie, and green shirt of the police force. A large man, he shook hands with even more formality than Bahr had done. 'I am honoured to meet you,' he said in slow, stilted English.

'Now, do sit down, Herr Alvarez.' Bahr indicated the armchair set in front of the desk. Once they were all seated, he said: 'I have your formal written request here.' He tapped a paper on his desk. 'But before we consider it in detail, would you care to tell us as much about the background to the request as you consider relevant?'

Alvarez opened his briefcase and brought out a couple of sheets of paper on which he'd made notes and then, occasionally referring to them, he outlined the case and his reasons for believing that the jewels and the gold plate were in a safe deposit somewhere in Liechtenstein.

'I'm sure you will have brought a document to prove that these things were stolen?'

'Yes, señor.' Alvarez returned to the briefcase and brought out a letter in an unsealed envelope. 'This is from my superior chief, witnessed by a notario who has affixed his seal. I think you'll find it satisfactory.' He stood to pass the letter across the desk.

Bahr read the letter, skimmed through the accompanying list, then handed both to Goppel. He waited until Goppel finished reading, said: 'This is perfectly straightforward, isn't it?'

'Yes, Herr Bahr,' Goppel said. 'We are able to accept without any reservations that the jewellery and listed gold plate are stolen.'

'Good. Now, Herr Alvarez, will you identify the person who will be making the withdrawal and the bank from which he will be making it?'

'I'm afraid I can't.'

'Oh!'

'But I can say that the attempted withdrawal will be made on either the nineteenth or the twentieth: that is, tomorrow or the next day. So if a watch is kept . . .'

'Please, one moment.' Bahr paused, as if he wished to choose his words with even more care than usual. 'You do understand that our banks operate under very strict measures of security—that is, customer security?'

'Yes, indeed.'

'This means that we are forbidden, by law, to disclose any details concerning bank accounts or deposits to any third party unless and until two requirements are met. First, the reason for such disclosure is that a criminal activity has taken place and the money or articles in question are the proceeds of that criminal activity: second, that the person and the account or deposit are positively identified. The first requirement has clearly been met by you; regretfully, I have to say that the second has as clearly not.'

'Señor, if the murderer goes to the bank . . .'

'If?'

Alvarez silently swore. Did this man of ice have to keep underlining the obvious—that Inspector Alvarez still didn't know for certain what in the devil had been going on? 'Señor, if the murderer goes to the bank, the very act of withdrawal will identify him.'

'Naturally, I appreciate that. But the fact is, is it not, that I am by law obliged to ask for an identification from you before I may advise the Commissioner for Banks that he should request the Commission to instruct their members to cooperate, while you are asking for our prior cooperation not only to discover whether such an event does take place but also, if it does, in order to make that identification?'

'If . . .'

'Let me first say this. My sympathies are with you, but my hands are tied. The law is quite unambiguous.'

'But there's always a way round the law, isn't there? I mean, suppose you were to have a quiet word with one or two people . . .'

'Please.' Bahr held up his hand. He sounded hurt, as if his character had just been put in question. 'My terms of reference are precisely laid down by the Diet and I am quite unable to move beyond them.'

Alvarez spoke urgently. 'It's been an impossibly difficult case: but at least there's now a chance to determine the truth. If in the next two days no one tries to withdraw the treasure, then the murderer is dead, having committed suicide. On the other hand, if someone does try, that someone is the murderer who's killed again and again from the basest of all motives, a lust for money . . .' He became silent as he realized that it might have been more tactful not to have used such words in the present company.

Bahr said to Goppel: 'Commissioner, would you agree that, unfortunately, there is no action that we may take in this matter?'

'Indeed, Herr Bahr, no action whatsoever.'

Bahr turned to Alvarez. He remained polite, but it was now not a cold but an icy politeness. 'Herr Alvarez, unless you can positively identify the man who will be making the withdrawal, I have to refuse you any form of further cooperation.'

CHAPTER 24

'The case is a pyramid of impossibilities,' muttered Alvarez in Spanish.

'Sir?' said the barman in English.

'Just reporting to my superior chief . . . Give me another brandy, please.' He pushed his glass across the bar.

He wondered if Herr Bahr, honest Herr Bahr, realized

what an appalling hypocrite he was? Goddamn it, if he'd had half a litre of blood in his veins instead of ten litres of frozen assets, he'd have agreed to turn a blind eye to the rules . . .

The barman interrupted his gloomy thoughts. 'A brandy, sir. Some gherkins? We build a new factory which exports tinned gherkins to many countries, including even Germany.'

He ate a patriotic gherkin. He drank the brandy. Either tomorrow or the next day, a man might turn up at a bank or strong-box depository, identify himself, be taken down to the strong-room, and collect the fortune. Then he'd be away, never dreaming for one second that he'd so nearly been trapped—would have been if only this had not been a country where rules were held to be so much more important than their consequences . . .

The barman mistakenly thought Alvarez's dejected expression meant that he was bored and would welcome conversation. 'Do you enjoy the visit to our lovely land, sir?'

'Not when I have to spend my time bashing my head against a brick wall.'

'Sir?'

'Something was impossible, yet it might well have happened. Now I'm faced with something equally impossible, but I've got to find a way of making it happen. How?'

The barman was a very serious young man who studied English during his off-duty time because he believed that anyone with ambition should be able to speak at least three different languages. 'Sir, maybe I do not understand. Because if something is impossible it does not happen: if it does happen, it is not impossible.'

Alvarez thought about that and after a moment he said suddenly: 'My God! Turn it upside down and it looks the right way up!'

'Yes, sir,' said the barman, again not understanding what was being said and gloomily coming to the conclusion that English was a more complex language than he had thought, but polite to the end. He moved away to serve two other hotel guests.

Alvarez picked up another gherkin and slowly nibbled at it. Throughout the case, he'd viewed events, as he'd naturally been taught to do, in their known and logical sequence. Clarke and Allen had died and a possible connection between the two deaths had appeared. Short died and the connection was confirmed. Marsh died and his murder identified Massier as the murderer. So when Massier died he, by elimination, must have committed suicide even though there were one or two facts which didn't quite fit the pattern . . .

Now turn everything upside down. Start with the premise that Massier had been murdered. Then the impossibility occurred before his death. But now, by definition, it couldn't be an impossibility . . .

Goppel's office was smaller and much less luxuriously furnished than Bahr's, but it possessed the same degree of clinical neatness. Not even a single sheet of paper lay out of place on the desk. Alvarez mentally compared this room with his own back on the island and he wondered if Goppel ever found life rather cold?

'Do you wish a cigarette?' Goppel rose from his chair and leaned across to offer a slim silver cigarette case. He grunted as the edge of the desk dug into his generous stomach.

When he was once more seated, and smoking, he began to drum on the desk with his fingers. He looked at his watch for the third time in less than a quarter of an hour. 'The banks soon are closing for today.'

'I know.'

'And we are the second day.'

So what else is glaringly obvious? wondered Alvarez. They'd spent much of the past two days in each other's company and if this had taught them nothing else, it had taught them that they'd little in common: every conversation had become stilted as they'd both struggled to keep it going from a sense of politeness.

The telephone rang. Goppel answered it. Certain it was just one more routine call, Alvarez stared through the window at the distant view of the Schloss Vaduz, set high on its crag: a view he'd come to know all too well. Then a sudden change in Goppel's tone of voice caught his attention.

After a moment, Goppel replaced the receiver. 'He is arrived, Herr Alvarez.' He stood. 'We speak with him.'

The guardia car braked to a halt in front of the post in Llueso. 'The fare'll be three thousand two hundred,' said the driver cheerfully.

Alvarez, small suitcase and parcel in one hand, briefcase in the other, climbed out on to the pavement. 'I'll buy you a drink.'

'I'm still waiting for the one you promised me last time.'

'Never lose hope.' He crossed the pavement and entered the post, went up the stairs and into his office, to find it stuffy and swelteringly hot. He crossed to the window and opened it, but left the shutters closed. He crossed to the desk and sat. He must report to Salas, who would have to set in motion a request for extradition . . .

He put his feet on the desk and tilted the chair back. How to explain things to Salas? How to gloss over the fact that he should have divined the truth long before he had? After all, as the barman at the Hotel Rheineck had indirectly pointed out, there had been one unshakable truth throughout the case — if something happened it could not be impossible.

The murderer had had to benefit from his murders or

there was no motive for them. Since Massier was the last to die, he could not be the murderer. That left Clarke, Short, Allen, or Marsh. They were all dead, so it was impossible one of them could be the murderer. But since one of them had to be, one of them was not dead. Clarke's body had been identified by Tracey, Short's by his fingerprints, Allen's by his wife, Vera, Marsh's by his boyfriend, Guichard. Tracey, Vera, or Guichard could have been lying: only the fingerprints could not lie.

Tracey had not been really distressed by Clarke's death. Had she deliberately become friendly with the investigating inspector in order to learn whether there were any suspicions that it had not been Clarke's body which she'd identified? And when finally satisfied, had she then left him to return to Clarke and enjoy the waiting fortune? But although she was emotionally selfish, surely she loved life far too much ever to assist in murderously taking it?

Vera Allen had been shocked by the death of her husband and totally bewildered by the awful problem of how she was going to survive financially. Surely the most consummate of actresses could not have simulated her grief and bewilderment?

Guichard and Marsh had had a row because Marsh had, correctly, believed Guichard was friendly with another man. In such circumstances, would Marsh ever have accepted Guichard as his accomplice?

If the corpse had not been that of the man reported dead, whose corpse had it been? There'd been no report from anywhere on the island of a missing man.

So none of them was the murderer. And Short couldn't be the murderer because his body had been identified by his fingerprints and it was impossible for a fingerprint to lie . . . But if the murderer wasn't one of the other three, then it had to be Short . . .

Charles Prade had arrived at Palma airport on a

package tour. The couriers had, as usual, been standing immediately outside the luggage lounge and as the passengers came through they'd picked out all those who were booked with their respective firms—either because they were approached by the passenger or from the labels on the suitcases—and had directed them to the appropriate buses. Prade had spoken to Caroline Brown to tell her that his friend, Peter Short, had unexpectedly met him at the airport, was going to take him home for a drink, and would then drop him at the Hotel Don Emilio. The fact that when he'd spoken to Caroline he'd seen Short showed that he must have already passed her once, when he had left the luggage lounge. In other words, she did not identify him as Charles Prade until after he'd met Short . . . It had, of course, been Short who'd gone up to her and identified himself as Prade after leaving Prade in his parked car, totally unaware of the deception that was being played out. On the face of things, this might have been a dangerous moment if someone who knew him as Short had seen him. In fact, there'd been little danger. It had been Prade who'd walked through the group of waiting people and so, naturally, no one had taken the slightest notice of him. Then Short had carefully waited to identify himself as Prade to Caroline Brown until she had left and was outside—a point where most people would be hurrying somewhere and not concentrating on who was around. And unless Caroline had at some time subsequent remarked that 'Prade' had come up and spoken to her and the listener had also been a watcher at the airport who'd known she was really talking about Short, then the switch would never come to light. In any case, Short had dyed his hair black and had worn large dark glasses and it was surprising how much these two small things could change a man's appearance if he were only briefly and incuriously seen.

Short had driven Prade to his home, Ca Na Rostra.

The house had previously been spring-cleaned from top to bottom by Juana Ortiz in order to erase all Short's fingerprints—not, of course, that she'd had the slightest inkling of this—and then Prade had carefully been induced to leave his prints where they would be found by anyone later seeking to confirm 'Short's' identity: on a glass, on a cupboard door, on a book jacket in the only occupied bedroom. Then Short had rendered Prade unconscious, carried him down to the port, shipped him aboard the chartered motor-cruiser, fixed a gas cylinder to leak, set a time fuse, and returned ashore.

He'd booked in at the Hotel Don Emilio in Cala Baston. Cala Baston was fifteen kilometres from Puerto Llueso and about the same distance from Llueso. Because it catered mainly for German tourists and because it was that far away, there wasn't much chance of someone from either Puerto Llueso or Llueso seeing him and identifying him as Short. But, just in case, he'd adopted the stratagem of saying he was suffering from an upset stomach to explain why he spent so much time in his room, didn't swim—that hair dye mustn't get washed out!—and never left the hotel.

When he'd been questioned, he'd naturally been shocked to learn about the death of Peter Short. He'd then given all the help he could towards the formal identification of the body, to the extent of mentioning the signet ring and the gold-backed tooth: he'd even given his fingerprints, albeit after a formal objection, because they would help to confirm the identity of the dead man. Then, at the end of the week, he'd flown back to the UK, after which he'd disappeared. So Charles Prade went missing, but since any investigation would immediately show he'd landed in the UK, inquiries would not be made in Mallorca: those investigating the death of Short would never learn about Prade's disappearance . . .

Fingerprints couldn't lie. But the circumstances surrounding them could. Two people had had drinks at Ca Na Rostra that night: Short and Prade. Prints of the dead man matched those on one of the glasses and those to be found in the occupied bedroom. So obviously the dead man had to be Short...

When Alvarez entered his home, Isabel and Juan started jumping around him and demanding to know what presents he'd brought them. He gave Juan three sets of Liechtenstein stamps, Isabel a doll in regional dress, Jaime a bottle of German brandy, and Dolores a headscarf. Jaime insisted, despite Dolores's objections, on opening the bottle to see how a German brandy compared with a Spanish one. Several comparisons later, the two men agreed that any differences were immaterial.

It was over an hour and half before Alvarez wandered into the kitchen where Dolores was slicing up an onion. She said: 'There's a letter for you, Enrique. By the coffee jar.'

He went over to the open shelves to the left of the cooker, and picked up the envelope. The stamp was an English one and the handwriting was spidery and slanting and the g's, f's, j's, p's, and y's, had exaggerated loops.

'Is it from her?' she asked.

He nodded.

'Mother of God, if only you'd never met!'

He said slowly: 'Then a murderer would have got away with five, perhaps six, murders and a fortune belonging to the Marqués de Orlocas's daughter.'

'And how did the Marqués amass his fortune?' she demanded violently. 'From the bloody sweat of people like you and me. Why should his daughter get it back?'

He shrugged his shoulders.

'Why should you have to suffer so much that the murderer gets caught?'

'I don't know. I don't know any of the answers.' He did not open the letter but tore it up into tiny pieces.